MW00966951

FAIRY METAL THUNDER

SONGS OF MAGIC, BOOK 1

by J.L. Bryan

Published September 2011
www.jlbryanbooks.com

Fairy Metal Thunder by J.L. Bryan
Copyright 2011 Jeffrey L. Bryan. All rights reserved.

The following is a work of fiction. Any resemblance to real persons or events is coincidental.

ISBN-10: 146635190X
ISBN-13: 978-1466351905

For John

More books by J.L. Bryan

The Paranormals Trilogy
Jenny Pox
Tommy Nightmare
Alexander Death

Helix
The Haunted E-book
Dominion
Dark Tomorrows

Chapter One

After school, Jason rode his bicycle across town to Mitch's house for band practice, with his guitar case strapped to his back. His palms coated the handlebars with nervous sweat. He'd spent the whole day ignoring his teachers while he furiously scribbled lines of the new song, crossed them out, and rewrote them. He'd accumulated three notebook pages' worth of jumbled, blotchy words, plus ink stains all over his fingers.

During sixth period Social Studies, he had very carefully copied these bits of song onto a single page, using the most legible handwriting he could muster. He'd titled the song "Angel Sky" and then hesitated a minute before writing "For Erin" underneath the title. Then he'd folded it into neat squares and tucked it in his pocket, where it now burned like a handful of hot coals.

He paused at the top of Mitch's street. He could see Mitch's house, four doors down, the garage door open and waiting for him. He could hear Mitch warming up on the keyboard, the fake piano sound echoing through the tree-lined neighborhood.

Jason's nerves were rattling. He'd never shown the group any of his songs. Erin was the singer and the songwriter of the group. Like Jason, she was a junior at Chippewa Falls High. Unlike Jason, she was actually talented at writing lyrics.

"Hey, little kid, need a ride?" a girl's voice asked. He jumped in surprise and nearly fell from his bike. While he was lost in thought,

Dred had pulled up alongside him in her beaten-up '97 Chevy van. She snickered at Jason. Dred was a year older, close to graduation. She was a broad-shouldered girl who liked Doc Martins and ragged plaid shirts.

"You're hilarious," Jason said.

"Race you!" Dred stomped her gas pedal until she was halfway down the street, then slammed her brakes and twisted into Mitch's driveway.

"Yeah, that's fair," Jason muttered as he pedaled down the street. Dred—or "Mildred" if you wanted to get punched in the face —was the band's drummer. She was a senior like Mitch, a year older than Jason and Erin. Her van was perfect for transporting the band to gigs. Hopefully, they would actually have a gig one day.

Jason turned into Mitch's driveway and parked his bike just outside the open garage. Dred was already there, juggling her drumsticks as she sat down behind her drum kit.

"Yo, Jason!" Mitch said. He sat at the keyboard, his long hair unleashed from the plaid driving hat he usually wore, and he pushed his John Lennon-style glasses higher on his nose. His t-shirt depicted ghosts chasing Pac-Man through a maze. Pac-Man's thought balloon read: "This is a stupid way to live."

Behind Mitch hung a poster of pop star Claudia Lafayette, in concert, wearing a pink dress and a headset with a microphone, pointing straight out to the audience while she sang. Mitch claimed the poster of the cheesy singer, whose bubble-gum songs could stick in your ear and repeat themselves all day long, was supposed to be ironic. He said the same about his Claudia Lafayette T-shirt.

"What's up?" Jason asked.

"Just stoking the flames." Mitch resumed playing his keyboard, switching it to a deep electric organ sound. "Making the magic happen, man."

Jason sat in a lawn chair and took his guitar out of the case. He plucked a few chords and tried to tune it, but couldn't hear anything over the keyboard.

When he looked up, he realized Erin had arrived, and his heart skipped. He gave her an awkward smile and tried not to stare. He thought Erin was beautiful, with her intense green eyes and blond hair dyed with blue and green streaks. Her hair was long and usually hung down all over her face. Jason always wanted to brush her hair back behind her ear so he could see her better.

He waved to her, but she'd already turned away to hang her jacket on a hook over the workbench.

"About time!" Mitch yelled over the noise. Then he realized he was the source of the noise and stopped playing the keyboard. "Where have you been?"

"Zach had to drop off a couple other people first," Erin said. "Chill out, Mitch."

"It's *Mick*," Mitch said.

"You can't be Mick. Mick isn't short for Mitch," Dred said. "It's for Mickey, or maybe Michael—"

"Don't tell me what nickname I can be...*Mildred*," Mitch said. "It's a free country."

"Don't call me Mildred!"

"Don't tell me I can't be Mick!"

"Okay, kids," Erin said. "Do you want to fight, or do you want to play?"

"Fight," Dred replied. She aimed a drumstick at Mitch's head.

"I'll be ready as soon as you admit that I can use 'Mick' for my stage name. It's really not that far from Mitch--"

Dred interrupted him with a short, loud drum solo, ending with a cymbal crash. Mitch scowled.

Jason tried to work up the nerve to tell Erin he'd written a song for her, but he couldn't seem to get his mouth working. Though he'd gone to school with Erin since her parents moved to Chippewa Falls back in ninth grade, he hadn't spoken with her very much at all. The sight of her always seemed to lock up his mouth, and his brain along with it. He'd been thrilled when Mitch asked Jason to join their band a couple of months earlier. According to Mitch, their previous guitarist had been "a total spaz who never showed up for practice."

Instead of talking, Jason strummed his guitar to warm up his fingers.

"Good," Erin said. "At least somebody takes this seriously."

"Let's go," Mitch said. He played his fingers across the keys, and an electrically synthesized piano buzzed over the speakers.

Erin blew a short tune on her harmonica, then spoke into an imaginary microphone.

"Hello, Wisconsin!" she shouted. Mitch played the sound of an audience applauding from his synthesizer. "We are the Assorted Zebras! Who's ready to rock?"

"Don't say that," Dred said. "It's cheesy."

"Just count us off, Dred," Mitch said.

"What are we playing?" Dred asked.

"This is a song I wrote for my boyfriend Zach," Erin told the imaginary audience. "It's called 'The Next Road Out of Here.'"

Dred tapped out a beat, and then Mitch and Jason joined in with the keyboard and guitar. The song started slow, with long, sad sounds from Erin's harmonica. Then she sang:

We've been in this town so long,
I forgot the world outside...
So let's escape tonight,
It's time to take a ride...

Then the song became loud and fast.

Let's run together
To that place where there's no fear,
The place we want to go,
The next road out of here!

Jason's fingers flew across his strings as the tempo accelerated. A few little kids from the neighborhood, three boys and a girl, showed up on bikes and scooters and sat in the driveway to listen, as they sometimes did. Erin smiled and waved, clearly delighted to have an audience, even if they were in elementary school and one boy was more interested in picking his nose than watching the show. Two of the kids were even nice enough to applaud when the song ended.

"Can you play some Weird Al?" the nose-picking boy requested.

"Yeah, do a Weird Al polka!" another boy said.

"We're just practicing our own songs right now," Erin told them. "Want to hear those?"

"Who cares?" the biggest boy asked. He rode away on his scooter, and the two other boys followed. The little girl remained, but rested her chin in her hand and looked bored.

"I've got something fun," Erin said. "It's called 'Cinderella Night.' Want to hear it?"

"I guess," the little girl sighed.

Dred tapped out four beats, then Jason and Mitch joined in. Erin sang the upbeat song about a girl sneaking out and meeting a boy in a nightclub.

The little girl smiled, entertained at last.

They played two more of Erin's songs. Jason tried not pay attention to Erin's hips swaying as she danced, or the pale stretch of her belly that sometimes peeked out over her low-slung jeans. He tried to focus on making the music.

Erin stopped halfway through the third song.

"We need to mix it up," Erin said. "It's all fast, dancey stuff."

"What we really need is a killer love song," Mitch said. "One of those everybody-get-out-your-lighter things."

"I don't have anything like that," Erin said.

"Maybe I'll write one," Mitch said.

"You? Writing a love song?" Dred snorted.

"Like you could do better," Mitch said. "Yours would probably end with the girl killing her boyfriend and burying him in the back yard."

"I think your songs are good, Erin," Jason said.

"Thanks, Jason, but Mitch is right. We need a good, slow love song. I just don't know how to write something like that."

Jason's hand dropped to his jeans pocket. The song was folded up there, "Angel Sky," all about falling in love. He hesitated, wishing he hadn't written "For Erin" underneath the song title. Everybody would laugh at him if they saw that. Erin would probably think he was a weirdo for writing a song for her.

"I'll be right back," Jason said. He put his guitar aside and walked toward the door into the house.

"Whoa, hold it," Mitch said. He stopped Jason with a hand on his elbow. "Where are you going?"

"The bathroom." Jason planned to find a pen inside the house and scratch out the dedication. Then he could show everyone the song without getting ragged on. Or at least, they'd pick on him a little less. And Erin wouldn't decide he was an obsessive stalker freak to be avoided.

"No way. My mom says nobody's allowed in the house when she's not home," Mitch told him.

"Since when?" Dred asked.

"She says some of her jewelry's gone missing or something."

"And she thinks we stole it?" Dred asked.

"Well, my mom didn't accuse any of you of stealing, exactly," Mitch said, but he glanced at Dred. "She just says nobody's allowed in the house if she's not home. She's doing the night shift at the hospital, so that's a long time. Jason, why don't you go whizz in the back yard?"

"Oh," Jason said. That wouldn't help. Jason doubted he would find a pen or marker out back.

"What's wrong?" Mitch asked. "Were you going to drop a number two?"

Jason felt his face turn red. Why did Mitch have to say something like that right in front of Erin?

"He was!" Dred said. "Look at him blush."

"I wasn't!" Jason said.

"Yeah, right," Mitch said. "Just hold it, man."

"I'm…" Jason realized he couldn't think of a single thing to say that would make this conversation less humiliating. He wished he could escape into a hole in the earth somewhere, and maybe never come back.

He was saved by an even worse turn of events. A red Mitsubishi Spyder pulled into the driveway with its top down. This was Zach Wagner, a senior over at the Catholic high school, who was best known for modeling in the "Plaidwear" section of the Fleet Farm catalog since he was thirteen. He had flawless skin, a haircut that probably cost a hundred dollars, and dark blue eyes. Erin's boyfriend.

Zach stood up inside his car and drummed his hands on the top of the windshield. He pushed his sunglasses on top of his forehead. "Let's go, Erin! Those orphans aren't going to entertain themselves."

"What's up, Zach?" Mitch waved, falling into suck-up mode at the sight of Chippewa's most famous male model.

"Yo, Mick! Dred! New guitar guy!" Zach gave a mocking little salute. "Sorry to take your singer away, but we've got a busy night of important stuff."

"You're leaving already?" Dred asked Erin.

"I have to. We're going to a benefit for Stuffed Animals for Orphans, over in Minneapolis. Zach says everyone else in the Minneapolis acting community is helping out." Erin gathered up her purse.

"He's not an actor," Jason said. "He's a male model."

"You can't go now," Dred said. "We have the audition next week."

"Erin! Yo! Orphans! Stuffed animals!" Zach shouted.

"I'm coming!" Erin grabbed her backpack.

"You guys want us to play at the benefit?" Mitch shouted to Zach. "Cause we could do that. We can just pack it up into Dred's van and follow you to the Cities."

"Um...thanks anyway, Mick!" Zach said, with a wink and a thumbs up. "Stuffed Animals for Orphans appreciates your support. In fact, if you guys want to make a donation, I'll pass it along. There are lots of orphans out there who don't have stuffed animals."

"Oh, that's a good idea," Erin said. "Does anybody want to donate?"

Mitch grumbled something under his breath as he took out his wallet and gave Erin a couple of dollars. Dred donated a five-dollar bill from her money clip.

Erin smiled at Jason as she walked toward him, holding out her hand.

Jason searched all his pockets. He came up with twelve cents.

"Sorry, I don't have more on me," Jason said sheepishly. That's me, he thought, no money and no car.

"That's okay. Thanks." Erin gave him a quick half of a hug. "I'll be back here for rehearsal tomorrow."

Jason watched her climb into the car with Zach, kiss him, and drop into the passenger seat. He felt a little despair as they pulled out of the driveway and drove away.

"You know, I like that guy," Mitch said.

Jason nodded. Everybody liked Zach, of course. Perfect Zach.

Chapter Two

Jason sat at the dinner table, where his father read the newspaper, and his six-year-old sister Katie was sculpting what looked like a hippopotamus out of her mashed potatoes.

"George, stop reading at the table," Jason's mom said as she placed a platter of bratwurst and sauerkraut on the table. "Katie, stop playing with your food. Can't we have a nice family dinner here?"

Jason helped himself to a brat and spooned mustard onto his plate.

"What's wrong with you, Jason?" his mom asked.

"What do you mean?"

"You look so sad."

"I'm okay." Jason shrugged and poked listlessly at the bratwurst. On the inside, he was beating himself up for not showing Erin the song, for being stupid enough to actually put her name on it, and for letting Mitch embarrass him in front of her. The song was still folded in his pocket, unseen by anyone.

"You know—George, would you *please* stop reading that paper? —we talked about you at the Lutheran Ladies meeting yesterday."

"Me or Dad?" Jason asked.

"You, Jason. Do you know Mrs. Dullahan, over on the east end of town?"

"The witch?" Katie asked.

"Katie! She is not a witch. She's just a very lonely old woman with nobody to help her. I can't believe you would say that."

"Everybody knows Mrs. Dullahan's a witch!" Katie said. "If you trick-or-treat at her house, she'll turn you into a toad."

"That is not true, Katie," Jason's mom said. "Don't say such awful things about people."

"She is scary," Jason said. "Kip Ericson threw a football over her wall one time, and it came back all flat and burned up."

"Kip Ericson shouldn't be harassing old ladies," Jason's mom said. "Anyway, Jason. She lives all alone in that big house of hers, and she's so elderly. It's obvious she's having trouble keeping up her yard."

"Good thing most of it's hidden behind that wall," Jason's dad commented, without looking up from the paper. "What you can see is an eyesore."

"She can hardly be expected to do yard work at her age," Jason's mom said.

"How old is she, anyway?" Jason asked.

"A hundred and fifty!" Katie volunteered.

"Nobody's a hundred and fifty, Katie," Jason's mom said. "But she's very elderly, and she clearly can't do for herself. That's why I decided to volunteer my capable yet unemployed son to go and help her around the house."

"You said what?" Jason asked, startled.

"Just little things," his mom told him. "Mow the lawn, trim those wild shrubs, maybe do something about all that moss on her wall."

"Those don't sound like little things," Jason said.

"She'll turn you into a toad!" Katie said.

"Katie, enough! Jason, it would be nice if you would do a few things to help out your elders. It builds character. The poor woman's completely cut off from everyone."

"Maybe she likes being cut off," Jason said. "How do we even know she wants help?"

"Why wouldn't she?" his mom asked.

"Anyway, I'm busy with school." Jason hated the idea of going to Mrs. Dullahan's house. Every kid in town learned to fear her. Terrible stories were whispered about her. Jason was old enough to know that she wasn't really a witch or anything supernatural, but he couldn't help feeling scared of her anyway.

"School didn't stop you from working at the car wash," his dad said. "Might as well find something useful to do with yourself, now that you quit your job."

"Dad, I told you, I only got that job so I could save up for my guitar. Now I don't need to work anymore."

"Must be nice," his dad said, returning his attention to the paper.

"I don't know what's gotten into you with that guitar," his mom said. "You hardly ever practice your clarinet anymore. You'll have to work a lot harder if you want to be first chair in the school band next year."

"I'm not too worried about that," Jason said.

"You'd better worry about it. That Laura Wu is going to be serious competition for you," his mom said. "I want to see you working hard."

"I don't really like the clarinet. I like the guitar."

"What's not to like about the clarinet?" His mom looked scandalized. "You used to love your clarinet."

"I wouldn't say I loved it."

"Well, I was first chair clarinet in my high school band," his mom said. "If I can manage it, you can, too. And your father's right, we can't just let you loaf around with your friends all summer."

"We're not loafing, we're rehearsing."

"What you're not doing is *working*," his dad said. "You know, at a job? If you want to come to Bill's House of Tractor with me, Bill might be able to find work for you." Jason's dad sold farm equipment at Bill's, a large retailer in Eau Claire.

"Um..." Jason said. The idea of having his dad for his boss wasn't quite as terrifying as the thought of going to Mrs. Dullahan's house, but it was up there.

"Why don't you drop by Mrs. Dullahan's tomorrow afternoon?" his mom said. "Introduce yourself and volunteer to help out? That would be so nice."

"She'll probably think I'm trying to scam her."

"A nice young man like you?" his mom asked. "Besides, you'll be bringing one of Dotty Schuler's famous muffin baskets. That should settle any of her concerns."

"I can't tomorrow," Jason said. "We have rehearsal. There's an audition at The Patch in Minneapolis next week."

"Oh, I don't know," his mother said. "I don't like the idea of you going into the Cities with you friends. That's a rough area. You could get into trouble."

"There aren't any rough areas in Minneapolis," Jason said. "You make it sound like Las Vegas."

"Don't smartmouth your mother," his dad said.

"I'm not, Dad!"

"Don't yell at your father," his mom said. "I don't want to hear any more nonsense about this. You're going to Mrs. Dullahan's tomorrow, and you're going to be pleasant and useful."

Jason sighed and stirred his mashed potatoes.

Chapter Three

After school on Friday, Jason picked up a cellophane-wrapped, ribbon-topped muffin basket from Mrs. Schuler, who ran a small gift shop in town. He pedaled over to Mrs. Dullahan's, whose house was several streets away from his own, at the dead end of a road just outside town. It was atop a small hill, surrounded by huge old trees whose limbs gnarled together to form a dark canopy. The weeds under the trees were thick as cornstalks.

Jason rode his bike up the short length of driveway and stopped at the gate. A high brick wall, thick with moss and mold, blocked most of Mrs. Dullahan's lawn from view. He could see one wooden turret of her house beyond it, with its single narrow window shuttered tight.

The gate itself was a massive pair of wooden doors, inscribed with strange floral and geometric designs, and these were full of moss, too. The whole area around her house felt chilly, though the rest of the town was warmed nicely by the May sunlight. It was nearly summer.

A rusty metal box, with little speaker holes and a single unmarked button, was built into the brick wall by the gate. Jason felt uneasy as he pushed the button.

He stood there for a minute, waiting. Apparently, she wasn't going to answer, and that was a relief. He turned his bike around.

"Who's there?" a raspy voice clicked out from the rusty box.

"Oh!" Jason said. "Um, hi, Mrs. Dullahan. My name is Jason Becker. My mom and the Lutheran Ladies sent me over here." The lady didn't say anything, so he added, "Yeah...They said I should help you with yard work or something."

"Go away," the lady's voice replied.

"Okay," Jason said. "Should I just leave the muffin basket by the gate, or....?"

"Go away!"

"All right, sorry!" Jason started to put the muffin basket down, but then reconsidered. If the old lady didn't want it, he could bring it to band practice for everybody to eat. Maybe Erin would like that.

He pedaled to Mitch's house with the muffin basket dangling from his handlebar. Dred's van was in the driveway, and the garage door was wide open, but no music was roaring out.

"What's wrong?" Jason asked as he parked his bike just outside the garage. He set the muffin basket on the workbench. "Can't play without me?"

Mitch, Dred and Erin were in the garage, but they weren't touching their instruments. Instead, they were moving boxes aside and looking carefully at the floor, searching for something.

"I lost my necklace," Erin said. "The gold one with the little emeralds on the pendant? Have you seen it anywhere, Jason?"

"No, sorry. You lost it here?"

"I don't know. I've been looking everywhere." Erin's eyes were glistening like she was wanted to cry, but she was holding it back. "I've searched at home, at school, at The Creamery..."

"We'll find it," Mitch said. He looked around the base of the drum kit.

"I already checked there," Dred said.

"I'll help." Jason knelt and peered under the workbench on one side of the garage. He knew the necklace Erin was talking about. She wore it almost every day. It matched her green eyes. "When was the last time you saw it?"

"A couple days ago. I don't really remember."

"We've been looking for fifteen minutes. I'm pretty sure it's not here," Dred said.

Erin frowned and turned her face away from everyone. She crossed her arms. "Never mind. I'm sorry for wasting everybody's time. Thanks for trying."

"I'll check out in the yard." Jason walked outside to look over the driveway and the grass.

In the garage, Dred tapped impatiently on her drums.

"Thanks, anyway, Jason," Erin said. "Let's just play."

"You sure?" Jason asked. "I can keep looking."

"Nah, it's cool." Erin shook her head and tucked a lock of green hair behind her ear. "Forget I said anything, okay? We have to practice for the audition."

Jason took his guitar out of the case, which he'd left in Mitch's garage the previous night. "I meant to tell you guys, I can't come tomorrow night, either. I have to babysit Katie."

"That's two days in a row," Mitch said. "The audition is next week, Jason. I told you when you joined, you have to take the band seriously."

"I do take it seriously! My parents don't. I can't help it."

"You miss practice today, you miss it again tomorrow--" Mitch said.

"I didn't miss it today, though. Mrs. Dullahan didn't want me at her house any more than I wanted to be there." Jason held up the muffin basket. "Who wants a muffin? Erin, chocolate chip?"

"Thanks! I could use some chocolate." Erin smiled at him, and he suddenly felt soft and warm inside.

Jason punched through the cellophane and handed the muffins out. Mitch took both raspberry muffins and stuffed them in his mouth, puffing out his cheeks like a chipmunk.

"So, no more missing practice," Mitch said to Jason, spraying wet muffin bits as he spoke. "Got it?"

"I have to stay home tomorrow," Jason said. "I'll be lucky if my parents even let me go to the audition. My mom's still not sure. It's a school night."

"Dude, you're seventeen already," Dred said. "You should be able to go anywhere you want."

"Okay, just call my mom and tell her that," Jason said.

"You're not going to make the audition?" Mitch asked, looking alarmed.

"I'll make it. I can handle my parents. But that means staying home tomorrow."

"Work it out," Mitch said. "Don't miss another practice after tomorrow. And don't mess up this audition!"

"I won't," Jason said. He looked at Erin. "Are you feeling better?"

"Yep, don't worry about me. I'm the happiest girl in the world."
Erin said. She blew cheerful notes on the harmonica. "Let's play."

Chapter Four

Saturday night, Jason sat at home in his living room, his guitar in his lap, trying to pick out the music for "Angel Sky," the song he'd written for Erin. He was having trouble getting the music and lyrics to flow together.

His mother had dragged his father to a collectible ceramics convention in Minneapolis, an hour away, and they still weren't back.

"Jason?" Katie asked. She stood in the doorway of the living room in her Bert and Ernie pajamas.

"What is it, Katie?"

"Um..." She fidgeted, looking nervous.

"What's wrong? You should be sleeping."

"I know, but...there's a monster."

Jason sighed and put his guitar down. "Did you have a bad dream?"

"It's not a dream! I saw it go into Mom and Dad's room."

"If it's not in your room, you don't have anything to worry about."

"But I could be next!" Katie looked terrified.

"You're completely safe, Katie. There's no monster."

"Is too!"

"Okay." Jason stood up and stretched. "Let's go check it out. I'll show you there's nothing to be scared of."

"Thanks, Jason." She took his hand as he walked toward the

steps, something she hadn't done in a couple of years. She really was frightened.

They walked upstairs and to the end of the short hall in their split-level house. Katie stayed back, clinging to the frame of her bedroom door, while Jason approached the master bedroom.

"See, Katie?" he said. "Mom and Dad's door is still closed. How could a monster get into their room?"

"He just went puff," Katie said.

"He went puff, huh?" Jason said. He had no idea what that meant, but Katie had a very busy imagination.

Jason pushed open the door to his parents' room and glanced inside. "See, Katie, there's no...."

But Jason *had* seen something. He looked again.

There it was—a small creature, about two feet high, standing on his parents' dresser. It looked like a tiny person, dressed in a ratty, dirty wool overcoat, with a woolen cap pulled low over its eyes. Its pudgy green hands pawed through his mother's jewelry box. Jason watched the creature drop a pair of ruby earrings into a pocket of its coat.

"Hey!" Jason said.

The little creature jumped and spun around to face him. Its face was green and ugly, with an underbite, its eyes big and yellow under the low bill of the cap.

"What are you?" Jason asked.

The thing growled a little, then disappeared in a puff of green smoke. It reappeared in the space in front of the dresser, near the bottom drawer, and landed on its feet, which were clad in small, badly cracked leather shoes. It ran across the carpet to the window. It disappeared in another green puff, then reappeared standing on the windowsill.

"Stop!" Jason yelled. "Give that back!"

The little creature stuck out its dark green tongue at Jason, then disappeared with another puff of smoke. It reappeared on the little ledge outside the window, waved at Jason with a smile full of yellow, crooked teeth, and then hopped out of sight.

"Hey!" Jason ran to the window and opened it. He saw the creature blink in and out of visibility as it tumbled to the back yard, leaving a trail of green smoke fading in the air.

Jason hurried out of his parents' room, past Katie, who was crouching behind her door, poking out her head.

"Did you see the monster?" she whispered.

"Don't worry, I chased it away." Jason started down the steps. "But it stole some jewelry from Mom. I'll go get it back."

Katie stepped out of her room and walked to the top stair. "Can I come?" she asked.

"No, Katie! Wait here. I'll be right back."

"But I want to come with!" Katie crossed her arms and pouted.

"No! I'm serious, Katie."

Jason ran through the living room and out onto their concrete slab of a patio. He saw the little green man trampling through a flower bed at the edge of the yard. The creature reached the neighbor's split-rail fence and puffed through it.

Jason raced to the fence and leaped over. When his shoes hit the ground, the creature turned its green face to look back at him, snarled, and put on speed. It puffed in and out of sight, jumping forward about a foot each time.

Jason hurried to keep up as the creature shot forward across his neighbor's lawns. The little thing could move fast, but Jason had much longer legs than it did, and he gained on the creature.

He was determined to catch it, and not just to recover his mother's stolen earrings. If this little monster was the one who'd been stealing jewelry all over town, then it might have Erin's necklace, too. Jason could already imagine how happy Erin would be when Jason returned it to her.

He chased the creature into Mrs. Gottfried's yard, which was full of toy windmills and fake plastic birds. Jason caught up with it and reached one hand down to grab the creature by the scruff of its neck. Then the creature disappeared in another green puff, and Jason realized too late that the little monster had led him directly toward a low stone bench. Jason was running too fast to stop.

His shins cracked into the bench, and Jason spilled forward, falling among a family of plastic ducks.

Ahead of him, the little creature turned and laughed, revealing its crooked yellow teeth again. Its laughter sounded like a hyena.

By the time Jason scrambled to his feet, the green creature was across Mrs. Gottfried's lawn and puffing its way across the main road outside Jason's neighborhood.

Jason chased him through three more neighborhoods, activating motion-detector lights here and there when he came too close to a house. The little green guy seemed to have no effect on the motion detectors—they only clicked to life when Jason passed.

Then Jason chased him down an overgrown trail through the woods. The green creature reached a brick wall ahead, stuck its tongue out at Jason while waving the stolen earrings, then vanished in a puff of smoke.

Jason reached the wall and slapped his hands uselessly against it. The wall was ten feet high, covered in moss and mold. Jason realized it was the wall around Mrs. Dullahan's yard.

"Come back here!" Jason yelled. He thought he heard a hyena-ish giggle on the other side.

Jason picked one of the tall old trees next to the wall and climbed it as quickly as he could. He scrambled out on a thick limb over the wall, struggling to catch his breath. He'd been running nonstop.

Below him, the deep black shadows of Mrs. Dullahan's yard were scarcely pierced by the thin moonlight. It was inhabited by big old oak trees, almost as dense as a forest. The few patches of ground he could see were overgrown with tall weeds as thick as bamboo, and for a moment he was just glad he didn't have to mow her yard for her.

Then Jason saw a streak of weeds ripple, as if a rabbit were dashing between them.

He didn't have time to find a safe way down. Jason held his breath and dropped from the limb into the darkness below.

Something hard and wooden, the size of a shoebox, crunched under his ribs as he slammed into the ground.

Jason rolled up to his feet and looked at his aching side. He'd landed on what looked like a carved wooden squirrel, its mouth and eyes wide with fright. The fearful expression was heightened by that face that Jason had just broken its head from its body.

Looking around, his eyes adjusting to the shadows and moonlight, he saw more little wooden creatures—toads and rabbits and even a full-size deer. A wooden owl perched on a limb overhead.

All around him, little paths paved with moss twisted through the high weeds.

The paths snaked across the yard, curving across each other at little intersections. Each path ended at one of the giant old trees, at ornate little doors no more than a foot or two high, which appeared to be built into the tree trunks. He saw the little green creature scurry through an arched green door in a dark elm tree. It pulled the door most of the way shut.

Jason jumped after him, grabbing the tiny knob just before the door closed. The brass doorknob was the size of a child's marble in his fingers.

"Hey, come back!" Jason yelled. He pulled the door open, but the little green creature was nowhere in sight.

The interior of the tree was hollow. A series of roots formed a kind of staircase that spiraled down below the tree, out of sight.

"You're kidding," Jason said. He looked up at the dark shape of Mrs. Dullahan's house against the night sky. Maybe she wasn't a witch, but there was definitely something strange going on at her place.

Jason stuck his head into the open door. He looked up, into the hollow shaft of the tree, but it was completely dark.

Below, around the bend of the root-steps, he saw the slight glow of distant light. He could hear the faintest hint of music, and smell traces of wet, blossoming flowers and baking bread in the air.

He put his hands inside the tree and crept forward as far as he could. He scrunched his shoulders and squeezed deeper inside, looking a little further around the curve.

Somehow, he was able to fit even more of himself through the door, as if it expanded slightly for him. He crawled further down and around the root-and-dirt staircase, worried that the little green creature might pop out and hit him, or maybe bite him in the nose, but he was too curious to stop now.

The curving space seemed to widen even more as he crawled forward, so he could let his shoulders relax and spread out. He crawled down another twist of the steps, and then he was completely inside the tree.

The stairwell grew even wider as he moved forward on his hands and knees. The walls were made of packed dirt and more tree roots, and a few fireflies provided some light along the way. These fireflies were much larger and brighter than any he'd seen before, and their light was red and orange.

He crawled around and around, and soon the stairwell was wide enough for him to stand, though he had to almost double over, his back brushing against the ceiling.

He followed it down and down, around and around. Had it been a staircase in a building, he would have descended five or six stories by now. He kept going.

Finally, after hundreds of steps, he reached a door. He seemed to be standing inside the round shaft of the tree trunk, though he should have been deep underground now, far below the roots of the elm tree. Golden sap dripped along the heartwood walls. His hands were covered in the sticky stuff, and probably his shirt, which felt glued to his back.

The door in front of him looked just like the green arched door he'd entered above, except much larger. He would still have to duck his head to pass through it, but he wouldn't need to crawl.

Jason touched the brass doorknob, and then he hesitated. None of this made any sense. How could there be such a long staircase under the tree? And where could this door possibly lead? Was he going to be attacked by a bunch of angry little green creatures on the other side?

Then he remembered his purpose—recover Erin's necklace, and his mom's earrings, from the little green creature, who was probably still running away from him.

Jason took a deep breath and pushed open the little door.

Chapter Five

The door opened onto a cobblestone road curving through a dark forest. A number of the trees beside the road had little doors built into them. Jason turned and saw that he'd just emerged from a tree himself. He looked up along the trunk and saw it branched out into little limbs overhead, like a normal tree. Impossible. How could it be connected to the tree in Mrs. Dullahan's yard?

It was nighttime, but the forest was illuminated by swarms of fireflies, which glowed in a bright spectrum of winking colors— shimmering gold, fire-red, sunset orange.

He stepped onto the road, and a wooden cart came clattering around the bend. It was drawn by a pair of shaggy blue goats, and driven by what looked like a small girl with long sapphire blue hair that streamed out behind her like a cape.

"Out of the way, road-troll!" she shouted, and Jason scrambled back off the road. As she rocketed past, he thought he saw a pair of waxy, gossamer wings protruding from her shoulder blades. Little glass bottles full of frothy blue milk gleamed in the cart behind her, packed into place with golden hay.

Jason watched her clatter away around the next bend. She passed a low figure in a ratty woolen coat and hat, who strolled along the side of the road. It looked exactly like the little green man Jason had been chasing, only it was three or four feet tall now. Clearly, the creature believed it had escaped Jason. It was even whistling while it walked.

Jason ran up behind it. The creature heard his footsteps and looked back with a smirk, but then it gasped and its yellow eyes widened when it saw Jason. The creature lowered his head and began to run.

"Stop!" Jason yelled. He grabbed the creature's arm, turned it around to face him, and then lifted it up by its shoulders.

"You can't be here!" The creature struggled in his grasp, kicking at Jason's chest and stomach. "You must go back!"

"Where are we?" Jason asked.

"You don't know?" The creature breathed a sigh of relief. "Good. Good. Just go back and forget all that you've seen."

"No. You stole something from my house."

"Ah, yes." The creature reached into one of the many pockets in his coat and brought out the ruby earrings. "There you are. Now take them and leave. Go back through the same door. Your life is in danger as long as you're here."

"And the necklace," Jason said.

"Necklace, necklace...I don't believe I took a necklace from your house, young sir."

"Erin's necklace. Gold and emeralds."

"Doesn't ring a bell."

"You know you stole it from Erin a few days ago," Jason said. He gave the little creature a shake. "Give it back."

"Yes, yes! Anything's possible. Just put me down so I can check my pockets."

"Forget it."

"I won't run!" The creature gave a toothy, yellow smile, as if trying to appear innocent. "I swear it by the Sacred Cesspool of Gorbulorgh."

"The what?"

"The ancestral homeland of goblins!" The little creature looked at him indignantly.

"You're a goblin?" Jason asked.

"Naturally. What did you think?"

"I don't know...a leprechaun?"

"Leprechauns! I spit on leprechauns! I tie their shoelaces together to make them trip and fall! Leprechauns, indeed!"

"Just give me her necklace."

"As I said, I cannot search my pockets in my present position.

You must put me down."

"Don't even think about running again."

"I had truthfully not considered it, young sir."

Jason carefully set the goblin on his feet, but held tight to the collar of his coat. The goblin reached into various pockets, pulling out rings, jeweled broaches, golden watches.
"Necklace...necklace...ah! There you are!"

The goblin held out a silver, heart-shaped locket.

"That's not it," Jason said. "It's gold, with emeralds, like I said."

"So picky!" The goblin pulled more shiny objects out of more pockets. "I don't seem to have such a thing. I do apologize, young sir."

"Where is it?"

"I must have added it to my stash-hole at home. Are you sure you wouldn't prefer a nice diamond bracelet instead?"

"I want that necklace," Jason said.

"Understood, understood," the goblin said. "Allow me to make an offer. You return home the way you came, and never speak of what you saw here. Tomorrow night, I will return this necklace to your home."

"No. I want it now."

"That's not possible!" the goblin said. "I cannot take you with me into Sidhe City. The Queen would have me killed for leading a human here. And you too, for entering her realm uninvited."

"I'm not letting you go," Jason said. "I'm not stupid. I know you'll never come back."

"I am insulted, young sir."

"Just take me to where her necklace is. I'll leave as soon as I have Erin's necklace in my hand, okay?"

"It would be better if you waited here," the goblin said. "Hide behind those trees. I'll be right back."

"You're not getting away from me," Jason said.

The goblin sighed and slumped his shoulders. He looked ahead on the road, in the direction where he'd been walking.

"Slouch," the goblin said.

"What did you call me?"

"I'm telling you to slouch. Make yourself shorter. Snarl up your lips and try not to look so...human. You don't want everyone in the city staring at you."

"I shouldn't look *human*? Where are we, really?"

"Your kind call this the Otherworld."

Jason gave him a blank stare. "What are you talking about?"

"Annwn. Tir na nŎg. Faerie. Am I jingling anything loose yet?" the goblin asked.

"Fairies? Like little people with wings? That's crazy..." Jason thought of the small woman with the translucent wings who'd just driven past. "Are you serious?"

"Obviously, you know nothing of fairies," the goblin snorted. "Or you would show more fear."

"We're talking about little people with little wings, right? Like in Peter Pan?" He pointed ahead. "You're saying that girl was a *fairy*?"

"The most fearsome creatures in the realm," the goblin said. "It's why they get to name the realm, you see?"

"Whatever." Jason shook his head. He couldn't imagine little pixies with colorful wings as dangerous. The goblin was obviously just trying to scare him. "Let's get going. I need to get back home."

"More than you know," the goblin said. He began walking, and Jason stayed close beside him in case he tried to run.

"What's your name?" Jason asked. "Do goblins have names?"

"We have names!" the goblin snapped. "I am called Grizlemor the Cranky. And you?"

"Jason."

"Just Jason?"

"Jason the Guy Who Wants That Necklace Back."

The goblin sighed again. "When we reach the city, look no one in the eye. Say nothing. Just keep behind me and try not to draw attention to yourself."

The road led them to a great mound of a city, where the buildings were made of stone and live trees with sprawling roots and limbs. The city was arranged in terraces rising up the hillside. High above them, the top of the hill was encircled by a towering wall built of golden hexagonal bricks.

"What's that?" Jason asked, pointing to the huge wall.

"Don't point!" Grizlemor slapped Jason's hand down. "It's rude. That is the Queen's palace. We want to stay far from there. Don't even look in that direction."

"Okay, calm down," Jason said. "You really are cranky."

They walked under a high stone archway carved with the images of flowers and animals. As they stepped into the city, the cobblestone road beneath their feet turned into a street of brightly colored crushed pebbles.

Big swarms of fireflies lit up the city in red, golds, oranges, blues and purples. The stone and living-tree buildings all had round, curving shapes—he didn't see a square corner or a straight line anywhere.

Though it was nighttime, the fairy creatures crowded the city streets, and Jason saw long pastel hair and colorful transparent wings everywhere he looked. The fairies were selling flowers, jewels, rugs, shoes, pottery...all of it strangely small, designed for these people who stood no more than three to four feet high. Cheerful music played everywhere, strings and flutes and bells.

While most of the city dwellers appeared to be fairies, Jason also glimpsed other kinds of creatures mixed in here and there—little people with animal horns, or tusks, or long, pointy ears. He felt dizzy at all the strangeness, and he stooped over as far as he could so he didn't stick up above the crowd. He kept close behind Grizlemor.

"This way! Hide!" Grizlemor snapped, grabbing Jason's arm. They ducked behind a cart full of small, polished hand tools made of stone and flint.

"Why are we hiding?" Jason asked. Grizlemor covered his mouth with a calloused hand that smelled like sour spinach, and then the goblin pointed.

A group of three male fairies stalked down the street, and the crowd parted to make room for them. Their faces were youthful, like all the fairies, but their eyes looked hard, dark, and old. They wore segmented black armor, with their wings jutting out the back. Long swords hung in black sheaths at their hips. They ate fruit and flowers from the merchants they passed, but they didn't pay for it. The merchants just looked down at their feet and let them take whatever they wanted.

"The Queensguard," Grizlemor whispered. "They'll kill us both if they see you."

"Ho there!" The tool-seller bellowed at Grizlemor. He was short and stocky, with a beard that nearly reached his belt. "What might I sell you today? We have the finest flints from the Valley of Gog, lovely stone hammers from the Caves of Dormundy--"

"Quiet, dwarf!" Grizlemor snapped. The three armored fairies approached them along the street.

"You'll not quiet me, goblin!" the dwarf replied. "Why, I'll speak all day of the fineness of these hand-crafted tools, good for all

manner of carpentry, masonry, sculptory, or makery! Only the best
stones, only the best--"

"Fine, fine, I'll buy one!" Grizlemor handed the dwarf a golden
ring from one of his pockets.

"Ah, the gentleman goblin would like to trade at last!" the dwarf
said. He sniffed the ring, licked it, then bit it with his wide teeth.
"And what is your pleasure today? I have chisels of the greatest
quality--"

"I don't care, just be quiet!" Grizlemor whispered.

"Perhaps your friend would like...." The dwarf's brow furrowed
as he stared at Jason. "What manner of Folk are you?"

"He's an ogre," Grizlemor said.

"An ogre! He's hardly ugly enough for that!"

"Among his people, he is considered the ugliest ogre of all,"
Grizlemor said.

The dwarf turned to face the three Queensguard fairies
approaching his cart. "And how might I serve you, great fairies of the
Guard?"

Grizlemor tightened his grasp on Jason's mouth. If the armored
fairies leaned too far over the cart, they would see Jason and
Grizlemor hiding there.

"Dwarves require a special license to sell inside the city walls,"
one of the Queensguard fairies said. "Do you have your paperwork
in order?"

"Oh, yes, sir..." The dwarf reached under the cart and patted his
hand across an empty shelf. "I'm certain I have the scroll here
somewhere..."

"There is a fine if you don't have your scroll," the Queensguard
fairy said.

"Of course, of course," the dwarf said. He held out the gold
ring that Grizlemor had given him. "Will this suffice for today?"

The fairy took the ring and inspected it. Then he closed it in his
fist, and the three black-armored fairies continued along the street.

The dwarf frowned at Grizlemor. "I suppose you'll want to
complete your purchase now."

"Forget about it," Grizlemor said. He stood and pulled Jason to
his feet. "Come along, young...ogre. We have business ahead."
Grizlemor led him along the street.

"Thank you, good sir!" the dwarf yelled after him. "This was my
best sale of the day! I would appreciate your repeat business, gentle

goblin!"

"Why won't he be quiet?" Grizlemor muttered under his breath.

The goblin took them to a quieter area of the city, where mossy stone walls lined the street. Little round wooden doors were built into the wall, only a few inches apart from each other.

Ahead of them, Jason could hear enchanting music, like nothing he'd ever heard before. It soothed him and energized him at the same time. He wanted to dance his way down the street.

"Here we are." Grizlemor approached one of the round wooden doors. "My very humble home. I shall check my stash-hole...where are you going?"

Jason had passed right by, barely hearing the goblin. The music drew him forward, as if it had taken control of his feet.

Grizlemor hurried to catch up. "We've just passed my house."

"What is that music?" Jason asked. He followed the curved street around until he saw the source of it.

Ahead of him, there was a small park full of wildflowers at the intersection of two curving streets. People danced at the middle of the park—and they didn't look like fairies, but normal people, between the ages of ten and twenty, boys and girls, all different races, all dressed in very different clothes. They danced within a ring of large, spotted mushrooms.

Four musicians sat outside the ring of mushrooms on a woven-grass blanket. A hairy orange creature, bigger than a normal man, pounded a hand drum. Tusks jutting up from his lower jaw kept his face in a permanent snarl. A pink-haired female fairy played a small silver harp inscribed with floral-shaped runes. A young man with goat horns and hooves blew into an instrument made of a row of hollow reeds, arranged from shortest to longest and lashed together.

The leader of the band seemed to be the fairy with dark, violet-streaked hair and a matching violet heart tattoo on her arm. She played a six-stringed instrument with a neck that bent sharply back toward her. Jason recognized this as a lute, a kind of medieval guitar. She sang as she played, in a language Jason didn't recognize, and her voice was beautiful. She walked among the other musicians, nodding in approval as they played.

"We've missed our stop, young sir," Grizlemor said.

"What's happening here?" Jason said. "That music..."

"Makes you want to join in the dance, doesn't it?" Grizlemor smiled with his blunt yellow teeth.

"Those people dancing aren't fairies, are they?"

"They are human children. Like you."

"I thought you said humans weren't allowed here."

"They've only come to dance. They stumble in, here and there, all over the world. Through fairy rings--" Grizlemor pointed to the ring of mushrooms "--and other little doors to Faerie. They dance until exhausted, then return home in the morning."

"Why?"

"Because they cannot help it. The music draws out their energy, and their energy recharges our magical atmosphere."

"Are the instruments magic?" Jason asked.

"All things in the realm run on magic," Grizlemor said. "Now, if we could go back and conclude our business, young sir..."

Jason continued to watch, hypnotized by the fairy music. His body swayed, and his feet moved, wanting to dance.

"I want to stay and listen," Jason said.

"You should come with me."

"Just a minute longer," Jason said.

The goblin sighed again. "Stay right here if you must. But do nothing to call attention to yourself. I will return with your necklace, and then *you* must return home."

"Sure, sure..." Jason said, barely able to pay attention to the goblin. The music was amazing, opening his heart, making him feel every emotion at once. He hardly noticed when the goblin shuffled away.

Then the dancers began to fall, exhausted. When they hit the ground, they disappeared. The kids faded from view until the circle of mushrooms was empty, and the musicians stopped playing.

Jason blinked several times as he remembered himself. For a minute, he'd been unable to think of anything but the music. He'd never heard anything like it, music that made him feel excited and blissful while it played, and then sad and lonely when it stopped. The instruments really must have been magic.

The lute-playing fairy lifted the strap from her shoulders and laid the lute down on the grass blanket. She stretched and said something to the band. The four of them walked across the street and into an open-air cafe, where they bought drinks served in large, cup-shaped yellow lilies. The two fairies and the little goat-man sat at a stained-glass table, in chairs made of delicate little strands of wood. The huge, hairy drum player had to squat beside them because his giant orange butt would have obviously crushed the fairy chairs.

Jason glanced behind him. Grizlemor was nowhere in sight, and he wouldn't be surprised if the goblin wasn't planning to return. There were countless little round doors packed in tight rows along the wall—Jason would never be able to figure out the one to Grizlemor's house.

On the other hand...he wondered what his band could accomplish if they had those magic fairy instruments to play. He imagined crowds of people entranced by the music, unable to stop dancing until they fell over from exhaustion. With the magic instruments, they'd be able to get gigs all over Minneapolis, maybe even play somewhere in Chicago. And that would make Erin extremely happy, probably more than any stupid necklace.

Jason strolled up the street to the little park, keeping his head low. He checked across the street, down the alley. Nobody in the band was looking this way. They looked pretty exhausted from their set.

Jason picked up the lute. It was carved from heavy, dark wood with runes carved all over the surface. The tuning pegs glittered like gold. Violet amethysts were embedded here and there in the soundboard, and instead of an open sound hole, it had three floral shapes carved under the strings. The lute felt warm and inviting in his hands, heating his fingers like sunlight.

He looked over at the cafe again. So far, nobody had noticed him. Even with all the fireflies, there was still some darkness in the city night.

Jason could barely fit the little lute's leather strap over his shoulder and neck. The instrument pressed tight against his back.

He picked up the drum, which was covered with more of the strange fairy runes, and also had a strap for carrying and wearing. The interior was hollow, so he placed the reed pipes and the little silver harp inside it. Then he slung the drum's strap over the opposite shoulder from the lute.

Jason glanced sideways towards the fairy cafe as he started back down the street. The fairies were chatting rapidly now, as if energized by their drinks.

He walked away feeling extremely nervous, but he resisted the urge to run until he was out of sight of the cafe. Then he took off down the street, going back the way he'd come, through the crowded market.

The theft wasn't such a bad thing, Jason reasoned, because obviously the fairies were using the instruments to take advantage of people. Luring kids down here, draining them of their energy, sending them back exhausted...that didn't seem like a very nice thing to do. What had the goblin said? The fairies stole young people's energy to help power their magic.

He followed the curving roads out to the stone arch, then really put on speed when he hit the cobblestone road through the dark forest. He ran past tree after tree with the little doors built into them, until he saw an arched green door in an old elm. It looked like the door through which he'd entered the world of Faerie.

Jason ducked and entered the door, and closed it tight behind him. He ran up the spiraling root-and-dirt staircase. The stairwell grew narrower, darker and more cramped as he climbed back to his own world.

Chapter Six

By the time he reached the small door at the top of the stairs, Jason was covered in a fresh layer of dirt. He pushed open the arched green door and faced an unexpected rush of bright sunlight. How could it be daytime? He'd only been gone a couple of hours, at most. It shouldn't be much later than midnight.

He poked his head out the door. It was definitely daytime, though still shadowy in Mrs. Dullahan's back yard. It wasn't early morning light, either, but the full brightness of midday or afternoon.

His parents were going to kill him.

Jason looked at the house. Mrs. Dullahan wasn't outside, thankfully, and the narrow windows were shuttered or hung with dark curtains. Maybe she wouldn't see him.

The tiny doorway didn't look big enough for Jason to fit through. He took the instruments off his shoulders, and he put the lute outside first, laying it carefully in the high weeds. Then he pushed the drum out, scraping it on both sides as he forced it out the door. He lay flat on the ground and just barely managed to squirm his way through the little doorway.

Once he was out, the door slowly swung closed, while both the doorway and the door itself shrunk back to their original, even smaller size, as if the doorway had stretched to let him out.

Jason got to his feet and brushed off leaves and dirt. He wondered how many hours had passed. He'd left Katie alone, scared of the "monster" she'd seen. How long had she been waiting for him?

He climbed one of the old trees and out on a limb over the wall, then switched to another tree and climbed down. The instruments were strangely heavy for their small size, and they'd already made his back and shoulders sore.

He trudged through the woods, feeling drained, eager to reach his own bed and collapse. He knew he wouldn't get it so easy, though, if he'd left Katie alone all night. He'd have to get yelled at for a long time before he could sleep.

Jason reached his back yard, and he stopped in the garage to hide the instruments. His dad had an old Corvette convertible under a tarp, which had been there about as long as Jason could remember. He tucked the instruments in the narrow space between the draped car and the garage wall.

Then he approached the door into the house, took a deep breath, and walked inside.

His father was in the living room watching a fishing show, and he immediately stood up when Jason walked in.

"He's back," Jason's father announced. Jason's mother came down the short flight of steps from the kitchen. Katie trailed behind her, looking scared.

Jason's parents stood together and glared at him.

"Um...hi," Jason said.

"Hi?" his mother said. "Hi? After what you put us through, all you can say is 'hi'?"

"I'm sorry," Jason said.

"Where have you been, Jason?" his father asked.

"And who were you with?" his mother asked. "And why are you so filthy?"

"It's really hard to explain," Jason said.

"I told you," Katie spoke up. "He chased after the monster. The burglar monster. Cause it stoled your earrings."

"Oh, yeah, I got your earrings back, Mom!" Jason took the ruby pair of earrings from his pocket.

"They're covered in dirt!" His mom took them from his soil-encrusted hand. "Why did you take these?"

"I didn't," Jason said. "It was--"

"The monster!" Katie interrupted. "The monster stole them and Jason brought them back. Like he said he was."

"Katie, go to your room," his mom said.

"Why am I in trouble? What did I do?"

"You're not in trouble. Just go."

"But, the monster--" Katie began.

"Listen to your mother, Katie," his dad said. "We need to have a talk with Jason."

Katie frowned and stomped up the stairs to the kitchen.

"You still haven't told us where you were," his dad said.

"I was in the woods. A guy stole Mom's earrings, and I chased after him, and..."

"And what?" his mom asked.

"Then I got them back."

"From where?" his dad asked. "Who was this person?"

"It's really hard to explain. Can I just go to bed? I'll try to explain later."

"You will not 'just go to bed,'" his mother said. "We were worried sick. You left your cell phone here, too, so we couldn't call you. Were you with those wild kids from that band again?"

"They aren't that wild," Jason said.

"Mildred Zweig?" she asked. "And the Schneidowski kid? That Kavanagh girl, with all the weird colored hair? What's that hair about, if she's not wild?"

"How wild can you get in Chippewa Falls, anyway?" Jason asked. "Wearing plaid socks that don't match? Ordering the Tutti Frutti ice cream at The Creamery, just because nobody else does?"

"Don't be a smartmouth," his mom said. "What were you thinking, leaving your little sister alone like that? Don't you know she was terrified when we got home?"

"No, I wasn't!" Katie shouted down the stairs. "Cause Jason got rid of the monster!"

"Katie, go to your room!" his father shouted. "Jason, you're grounded. Obviously."

"For how long?" Jason asked.

"We'll talk in a month."

"But I have band practice. And our audition is Thursday--"

"You are not going to Minneapolis with those kids!" Jason's mother said. "Not after disappearing all night like that!"

Jason still couldn't understand how time had flown by so quickly.

"I don't want to hear anymore about this band nonsense," his dad said. "As soon as your final exams are over, you're getting a summer job. You need something to keep you busy."

"But I have to at least go to the audition with everybody," Jason said.

"Jason, no," his dad said. "Not one more word about it."

"But they're counting on me--"

"You should have thought of that before you decided to leave your sister alone and spend the night out with your friends," his mom said.

Jason realized it was pointless to argue anymore. If he told his parents he'd chased a goblin to the fairy world, he'd probably just get grounded even longer. And sent to a psychiatrist.

"Now, go and wash up," his mom said. "You're dripping dirt all over my carpet. And stay in your room while we rest. We were up all night worried about you."

Chapter Seven

Though he was very tired, Jason couldn't get to sleep Sunday night. He kept looking at his window, waiting for something to crawl through into his room—Grizlemor the goblin maybe, or a violet-haired fairy with a heart tattoo, or the hairy ogre-creature that played the drum. He jumped every time the wind made the trees creak outside. He was still awake when his alarm went off for school.

Monday morning, Jason left the house through the garage. Before he left, he peeked behind the old Corvette and lifted the drop cloth he'd used to cover the stolen instruments.

What he found surprised him. All four of the instruments had shrunk in size until they looked like toys. The lute was smaller than a violin, the harp would have fit in the palm of his hand, and the set of reed pipes was no bigger than a whistle. The drum was the size of a cupcake.

Jason could just imagine how Erin, Mitch and Dred would react if he brought these to school and suggested they use them to make music. They would laugh at him, or think he was crazy, or both. What had seemed like a brilliant idea in the land of Faerie on Saturday night looked ridiculous in the gray light of a Monday morning.

He covered up the instruments again, got on his bike, and rode to school.

While he was changing out books at his locker before

homeroom, somebody grabbed his arm and he jumped, nearly losing his balance.

"Hi, Jason," Erin said. "Scared you, didn't I?"

Jason was surprised to see her—Erin didn't normally hang out with him at school. She had her own friends. The sight of her tied up his tongue. He was only just barely able to say her name aloud: "Erin."

"Why are you so jumpy?"

"I don't know. I didn't get a lot of sleep. Weird weekend."

She leaned against the locker next to his. "Aren't you excited about this audition? I was thinking about it all weekend, and I really think this could be the one. The place isn't too big, kind of a college crowd..."

Jason was nodding along. He couldn't really look at her and talk like an intelligent human being at the same time, so he focused on changing out his books. "Yeah," he said.

"Don't you have a good feeling about it? I feel something good's about to happen."

"I hope you're right." Jason didn't want to tell her that his parents had grounded him, and he wasn't allowed to be in the band anymore. He knew he should be honest, but he was afraid she'd be disappointed in him. Or angry. Or decide not to talk to him again.

"You're going to be at practice?" she asked.

"I don't know—my parents are kind of mad at me, they don't want me going anywhere—"

"But you can come out for the audition Thursday right?" She touched his arm and looked into his eyes. "Right? Are you feeling okay, Jason?"

"Just tired. Couldn't sleep," Jason said.

"Did you have bad dreams?"

"I did."

"I hate that. I get nightmares all the time." She squeezed his arm, and Jason felt his heart flutter. "I'm really glad you joined the band, Jason. I think it's working out great."

"Me, too," Jason said. His smile felt a little too wobbly. He could feel himself starting to blush, too, which only made him more embarrassed.

"Oh, there's Kennedy and Parker. I have to go." Erin backed away toward her friends. "So, I'll see you Thursday. If you can't come to practice sooner."

"Right," Jason said.

He watched her go, feeling his insides tremble. Why did he have to be such a dork around her?

Later, at lunch, Jason sat outside in his usual corner of the courtyard. The school lunch was some kind of soy-burger sandwich with brown mystery vegetables. He could see Erin across the way on one of the concrete benches outside the cafeteria doors, with Kennedy and Parker and assorted other friends. It seemed like a large group to Jason. How did you keep up a conversation with that many people?

"What's happening, brother?" Mitch asked, sitting down next to him. At school, Mitch wore his goofy plaid driving cap, with his long hair tucked behind his ears, and his John Lennon glasses. He looked in the direction where Jason had been gazing.

"Just thinking."

"She's a good singer, isn't she?" Mitch asked. "Songwriter, harmonica. We're lucky to have her."

"Yeah." Jason took a bite of his soy burger and was quiet for a minute.

"I know what you're worried about," Mitch said.

"You do?"

"It's a big audition, man. Out in the Cities and everything."

"Oh, yeah. About that. My parents say I'm grounded. I'm not allowed to go anywhere for a while."

Mitch's mouth dropped open. "Except for the audition, right? And if we get the gig..."

"They won't let me go. And they say I can't be part of the band anymore."

"Are you serious? We can't blow this audition, man. Dred was after that club owner for almost a month just to get us a shot. What's she going to say?"

"I know, but I can't."

"We can't get a new guitarist by Thursday!" Mitch slapped his forehead and closed his eyes. "They'd have to learn Erin's songs...or we'd just have to figure out some covers...You can't do this to us, man!"

"I'm sorry," Jason said. "I really want to play."

Mitch looked him over. "You know, let me tell you a secret, as a graduating senior to a just-finishing-up junior. Your parents can't *really* make you do anything. It's like an illusion they have over you."

"They'd be really mad if I went."

"And they'd get over it. You're not doing anything wrong, you know. We're not going to rob a bank here. Just play a little music."

"Which is exactly what they told me to quit doing," Jason said. "I'm supposed to get a job..."

"That's perfect!" Mitch said. "Get a job, make a little money...plus, you can pretend you're going to work whenever you want to get out for a while. Having a job makes you groundproof."

"Should I pretend I'm going back to work on Thursday?" Jason asked. "I can tell my dad I got my old job at the car wash again. Then I could get away for that audition."

"Now you're thinking, man!" Mitch said. "He wants you to go to work, so that's what you tell him. And it's not *totally* a lie. I mean, we're trying to get a job. A Friday night gig at The Patch, in the warehouse district? That's big. We could make a hundred bucks each."

"I don't know. I really don't like lying."

Mitch glanced at Erin across the courtyard. "Look, man, what would Mick Jagger do?"

"Mick Jagger?"

"Do you think he'd let his parents keep him away from a gig?"

"He's like seventy years old," Jason said.

"You're missing the point. Rock stars don't ditch out on gigs because they're grounded. You know what I mean?"

"Not even Justin Bieber?"

"Shut up about Justin Bieber. This is about what you need to do, Jason."

Jason looked over at Erin.

"You don't want to disappoint her, do you?" Mitch asked.

"What do you mean?" Jason asked.

"You know what I mean."

Jason felt embarrassed. "Okay. But I can't make rehearsal all week. Just the audition."

"That's cool, man. Just keep practicing the songs at home."

"I'll practice." The bell rang and Jason stood up, feeling very nervous. He could get in a lot more trouble. He looked at Erin, and this time she saw him. She waved and smiled at Jason and Mitch.

"Get ready to play your best on Thursday," Mitch said. He punched Jason's shoulder. "Now you're acting like a rock star, Jayce!"

Jason rolled his eyes.

Chapter Eight

When school let out Thursday, Jason caught a ride with Dred from school, which meant riding around while she dropped off a couple of other girls that she always took home. He stashed his bike in the cargo area behind the back seats. When they reached Mitch's house, Jason parked the bike in Mitch's garage to make room for Dred's drum kit and Mitch's collection of keyboards and synthesizers.

Jason helped Mitch and Dred load the back of the van. He was doubly worried today. He'd told his dad it was his first day back at the car wash, and he'd been so busy wondering if he'd get caught by his parents that he'd almost forgotten to be nervous about the audition itself. Packing up the van, he started to think about playing in front of actual big-city club owners, and he felt a little cold and shaky.

Erin's boyfriend Zach dropped her off, and Jason looked away fast when she kissed him good-bye. Jason didn't need to feel jealous and sad, on top of everything else.

"Are we ready?" Erin asked as she joined them in the garage.

"All packed up." Dred tossed her keys in the air and caught them. "Let's go blow some minds."

As they drove out of Chippewa along Highway 29 to Minneapolis, Erin looked more cheerful than Jason had ever seen her.

"So where are you guys going to live when we're big stars?" Erin asked. "Dred?"

"I think Oregon," Dred said. "Seems like a cool place. You can live near those giant redwoods where they put the Ewok village."

"Mitch?" Erin asked.

"*Mick*. And I'm thinking Malibu. Swimming pools, movie stars..."

"Yeah," Dred snorted. "You only want to live there so you'll be close to Claudia Lafayette."

"I happen to think she's a great vocalist who does some amazing, experimental things with her melodies."

"I guess ten million middle school girls can't be wrong," Dred said.

"All kinds of people listen to Claudia Lafayette!" Mitch said.

"All kinds of female people between the ages of ten and fourteen," Dred said.

"What about you, Jason?" Erin asked.

"I don't really listen to Claudia Lafayette, or Britney Spears, or anybody like that. I like classic rock, old blues..." Jason said.

"I mean, where would you live if you were a rock star?"

"Oh!" Jason thought about it. "I think an island. Out in the Caribbean, maybe."

"That's pretty cool," Erin said. "But I think I'd want to live in New York, or London, someplace where everything's happening, and you can do anything you want."

"I could try that for a while," Jason said.

Erin smiled and blew a quick, bright tune on her harmonica. "Who wants to warm up?"

"My stuff's all packed up," Mitch said.

"I think I can play." Jason took the guitar from its case. He wished he'd brought the fairy instruments now, so they could at least check them out on the long ride to the Cities. He could have come up with some story about where they came from. Too late now.

Erin played a blues riff, and Jason followed her with his guitar. She improvised a song, continuing the harmonic part between the lines:

Jason likes the blues,
(wah-waah, wah-wah)
Mitch hates the news
(wah-waah, wah-wah)

"It's *Mick*," Mitch said. "But that's accurate, you know. I think it's pointless to get your news from the television, or even establishment newspapers--"

Erin sang and played:

(wah-waah, wah-wah)
Dred drives the car
(wah-waah, wah-wah)
Gonna take us far
(wah-waah, wah-wah)

"Yeah, where would this band be without my van?" Dred asked. Erin sang:

Without the van,
(wah-waah, wah-wah)
There is no band.

Erin played out a long phrase on her harmonica, while Dred snickered.

Jason and Erin played most of the way, occasionally getting into one of the band's actual songs, but Erin kept improvising new lyrics. She had a radiant smile today.

The Patch was located in the old warehouse district in Minneapolis, near a number of larger, more popular clubs. The club occupied one sliver of the bottom floor of a refurbished brick building, where the ghosts of the words "Great Northern Railway" were visible across the second story.

They arrived with about fifteen minutes to spare. It was still daylight—the club itself wouldn't open for several more hours.

The four of them walked to the front door. Jason wanted to knock, since the place was obviously closed, but Dred pushed open the heavy black door and walked inside like it was her own house.

"Hey, anybody here?" Dred shouted into the darkness.

Mitch looked at Jason and Erin, then shrugged and followed Dred inside. Jason and Erin shared a nervous smile before following.

The interior of the club was small and dark, with an eight-seat bar along one wall, scattered tables and a few booths at the back. The stage was tucked into one corner, and looked barely big enough to hold a two-piece band.

"We're closed," said a young woman who emerged from the door at the back. She was dressed in black leather pants and a high-collared white shirt.

"We're the Assorted Zebras," Dred said. "We're supposed to have an audition today."

"Oh, you're the one who keeps calling?" The woman turned her head and shouted at the open door from which she's emerged. "Hey, Freddy! Those pushy hick kids are here with their band!"

The man who came out next was hugely obese, wearing a bright flowered shirt and a green pork-pie hat. He stood next to the young woman and folded his arms while he looked over the four of them.

"Who's the one that keeps calling?" Freddy asked.

"That'd be me." Dred raised her hand.

"Well, stop calling. Lissa here is my entertainment director," he said, and the young woman smiled. "She's also my bar manager," he added, and the woman's smile faltered. "Anyway, this is your one chance to convince us that you're good enough to play The Patch. Go set yourselves up, and don't make too much noise doing it." He waved at the tiny stage.

"Thank you!" Mitch said. "We really appreciate this opportunity--"

"Don't talk to me until you're ready to play," Freddy said.

They carried the equipment and quickly set it up, plugging into the club's sound system. Freddy and Lissa sat in a booth at the back of the club, going over a stack of paperwork.

When they were set up, Erin spoke into the microphone: "Are you ready?"

Freddy the club owner waved a pudgy arm without looking at them. He was still in conversation with Lissa, ignoring the band.

"Okay," Erin said. "This first one's called 'Nuclear Morning.'"

Dred counted off the beat, and then Jason and Mitch joined in. Erin sang:

I woke up on nuclear morning,
Last night they gave the last warning,
Nothing left but crying and mourning,
All alone on nuclear morning...

They played three songs straight through, and neither of the two people in the booth looked up at them the entire time.

"Okay," Erin said, "This next one is called 'Remember'--"

"Wait, wait." Freddy pushed himself to his feet and waddled toward the stage. "Look, you seem like nice kids. You've got some talent." He looked right at Erin. "Maybe a lot of talent. But you're too green and raw. You don't have your sound together. I'd say give it another year of practice before you're ready to play live shows."

"A *year*?" Erin asked.

"Nobody gets successful overnight," Freddy said. "You're young. You have plenty of time to practice. Don't take it personally. Now get your junk off my stage."

Mitch frowned. Erin's face scrunched up for a second as if she were going to cry, but she fought it down and made it into a hard glare instead. The band members looked at each other. It was one more failed audition.

Freddy started chatting with Lissa again. After a second, he looked up and said, "Get going! We have a business to run here."

The four of them packed up their gear and carried it out to the van, speaking very little. On the drive home, the mood was quiet and somber.

"We'll get the next one," Mitch said as they drove out of the city. Nobody replied.

Back in Chippewa, Dred dropped Erin off at home. When the rest of them arrived at Mitch's, it was close to eight o' clock. Jason got his bike and his backpack from the garage.

He said good-bye and pedaled home.

His dad was waiting at the kitchen table, reading his paper. Jason heard his mom and Katie upstairs, doing something in Katie's room. Maybe cleaning up—Katie could turn any room into a wreck in a matter of minutes.

Jason poured himself a glass of milk.

"How was your first day back at work?" his dad asked, without looking up from the paper.

"Oh," Jason said. "Fine. Pretty good. I'm pretty tired now."

"Wash a lot of cars?"

"Yep."

His dad looked up. "You didn't wash mine."

"Oh...did you want me to?"

"I did. That's why I took it over to Manny's Car Wash this afternoon, about five-thirty. Guess who wasn't working there?"

Jason looked down at his shoelaces.

"In fact," his dad continued, "I talked to Manny, and he said you never even asked for your job back. Says he hasn't heard from you in a few months. Now how is that possible?"

Jason sighed. "I'm sorry, Dad."

"Where were you?"

"We had that audition today."

"You were with those kids? In Minneapolis?"

"It didn't go well."

"I don't care how it went. I told you no more band. And now you're going all the way to the Cities and back, with a teenage driver, and not telling anybody where you went?"

"It was a bad day," Jason said. "If that makes you feel better."

"It's not about how I feel, Jason. It's the way you've been acting. Disappearing all night? Lying to your mother and me? This isn't like you, Jason. What's going on with you?"

Jason shrugged. "I just like being in the band."

"You're getting irresponsible," his dad said. "You're going to be a senior next year. You need to start acting like an adult. Set a good example for your sister."

"Okay. I will."

"And why should I believe anything you say?" his dad asked.

"I don't know."

"You're still grounded, and you said you're not going to prom, so I'm running out of ways to punish you. And, at your age, it shouldn't be about punishment. You should be more mature. You should know to be honest, responsible and considerate of others. Especially your little sister, who you left all alone."

Jason didn't know what to say. His dad's disappointment filled the room like a thick, cold cloud.

"I'll do better, Dad," he finally said.

"I hope you do. Until you show me a little responsibility, I'll just think of you as somebody who can't be trusted at all." His dad started reading the paper again.

Jason trudged up the stairs to his room, feeling worse than he had in years. His parents hated him, and there would be no more band practice. No more afternoons and weekends with Erin.

He collapsed on his bed, put on his headphones, played the Lead Belly collection on his iPod, and closed his eyes.

Chapter Nine

Aoide slept in her woven-grass hammock, with the doors of her rear balcony open to catch the cool breeze through the trees. She was completely relaxed, her translucent purple wings stretched out to either side of her. When the fist pounded on her front door, she startled awake.

She fluttered her wings and hopped out of the hammock, landing gently on her bare feet. The fist pounded on the door again. "I'm coming!" she yelled. She yanked on a vine hanging from her ceiling, and the hammock folded up and pulled away into a knothole overhead.

Aoide opened the small porthole in her circular front door and looked out through the smoked-glass window. She could see out, but no one could see inside.

Her apartment was on the south trunk of a huge old sugar maple tree, the third door up. Like most fairy homes, she had a landing porch outside her front door. From there, a woven spider-silk bridge connected to the trunk's main walkpath. The walkpath itself alternated between more of the spider-silk rope bridges, little stairwells molded inside the trunk itself, and limbs trained to grow at just the right distance to serve as stairs.

Now, Aoide's view of the hustling, bustling walkpath was blocked by cold-eyed male fairies in black armor, with the Queen's Seal on their breastplates.

Aoide held her breath. This could be good news. She'd
reported their instruments stolen, and maybe the Queensguard had
found them. It didn't feel like good news, though. They weren't
carrying any musical instruments, either, just the iron swords in the
ornate scabbards at their hips.

Aoide lifted the smoked-glass window.

"Happy morning!" Aoide said. "I must have eaten a luck-clover,
to have three such lovely and handsome boys on my landing porch
today."

"You are Aoide the Lutist?" asked the Queensguard fairy who
stood closest to her door, in front of the other two. He had long hair
the color of polished gold and glittering sapphire eyes.

"I am she," Aoide said. "I certainly hope this is about the stolen
instruments. Did you find anything?"

"Her Majesty the Queen sends you this." He held up a black
rose in full bloom.

Aoide's fingers covered her lips, but she tried not to gasp or look
too frightened in front of them. A black rose could mean good
fortune or ill.

He held the rose close to her face, as if expecting her to accept it
on the spot.

"Oh, I cannot possibly go to court looking like this!" Aoide said.
"I'm still in my sleeping-dress. And my hair!" She put a hand to the
tangled violet-streak mess of her hair and backed away. "I'll be right
back! Promise!"

Aoide stepped back into her sleeping room and drew the
brightly painted dressing-screen across the doorway. She cranked her
music box to play a song while she got ready, and then opened her
rosewood clothes trunk and looked for a suitable dress. Then she
noticed her sleepy, unkempt self in the round mirror on the wall.
There wasn't time to fly over to the bath garden, but she needed to
wash up.

She stepped out onto her back balcony to collect fresh water
from her baby blue dew-pitcher flowers, and then gasped when she
realized someone had landed there. One of the Queensguard fairies
stood on her balcony railing with his arms crossed, quietly watching
her. He'd flown over to the back of her apartment, as if they
expected her to flee.

"Happy morning, good sir!" Aoide said. She tilted one of the
water-filled, pitcher-shaped flowers forward to rinse her face, then

brushed the water back through her hair. "Mind looking away while I dress?"

"My order is to watch this door," he said.

"This door, and not me, then?"

"Yes."

"Good!" Aoide slammed the pink shutters and slid the peg-lock into place.

She changed into her best dress, made of specially pressed and preserved violet petals. She stained her lips with a little elderberry juice, then raked her seashell comb through her hair until it looked sort of presentable. Then she pulled on her matching violet-petal slippers, since the Queen, joyless stickler that she was, insisted people wear shoes in her presence.

She stepped out into the front porch and smiled at the Queensguard fairy who'd first spoken to her. "I suppose I'm ready as I will be," she told him.

He held out the black rose toward her. Aoide steeled herself, then touched her finger to the bloom.

There was a smell like burning pitch, and then she and the Queensguard fairy stood in a small, hexagon-shaped side chamber of the Queen's court. The floor tiles were hexagonal, too. The tiles just below Aoide's feet depicted a large black rose.

Porting in through one of the black rose chambers was the only way into the palace. Most visitors ported in from the guardhouse at the outer wall, located where the front gate had been before the Queen ordered it sealed. Between the outer wall and the inner complex of palace buildings lay a vast labyrinth of deadly traps and foul monsters, which no one intruder could hope to survive.

"This way." The Queensguard fairy stepped out through an angular, arched doorway.

Aoide tried not to shiver as she followed him. She was terrified, but she didn't want anyone to see it.

They emerged into a great golden space that looked like an enormous cavern built of six-sided golden tiles, from floor to glittering roof. A thick swarm of fireflies radiated gold and purple overhead, where they lived on the pollen of flowering vines growing down from the ceiling.

Fairies came and went everywhere, dressed in their finest. Aoide and the Queensguard fairy walked up a long, wide carpet made of sewn-together rose petals, past groups of courtiers, ambassadors, merchants, costumed musicians and dancers, and more Queensguard men in their black armor. Tapestries depicted the Queen's past war victories, and the vast room was decorated with statuary and artwork from all over the realm.

Far ahead of them, at the end of the carpet, the queen's golden throne overlooked the room, atop staircases and terraces. From here, Aoide could see the glitter of her crown, and the theatrically huge skirts of her black and gold dress draped down over the terraced stairways beneath her.

Aoide was being led directly toward the Queen.

As they drew closer, Aoide could see the Queen better, her mountainous braids of midnight-black hair—which had to be a wig —sprawling over her dress like great pythons. The Queen surveyed her court with stern golden eyes and a beautiful, youthful face. Her eyes and lips were painted with black makeup, and a golden rune was painted on her cheek.

Aoide curtsied low before the Queen, nearly sitting on the floor before she rose up again.

"What have you brought me, Icarus?" the Queen's voice echoed down the terraces from her throne.

"This is the musician called Aoide the Lutist," the Queensguard fairy replied.

The Queen's head turned toward a silver-haired, bearded elf in a dark blue cowl, who occupied a terrace below her. He wore a golden chain, on which hung a pendant with a scarab trapped in amber.

"Conjurer," she said, "Create the Shush Bubble."

The old elf used a staff to heave himself to his feet. The staff was a crooked length of ironwood, topped with a gleaming quartz crystal. He muttered in Old Elvish, a language Aoide didn't know. The quartz ball sparkled, and suddenly all the voices, chatter and music in the room vanished.

Aoide turned around, half-expecting to find that everyone had disappeared. The courtiers were all still there, continuing their chatting and gossip, but it was as if an invisible curtain blocked all sound.

"Aoide the Lutist," the Queen said.

"Yes, Your Majesty?" Aoide replied.

"You reported to the Queensguard that four objects of high magic, four musical instruments, had been stolen from you. Yes?"

"Yes, Your Majesty." Aoide kept her gaze low, on the Queen's yards and yards of skirts. Subjects weren't supposed to look the Queen in the eye.

"Our seer tells us these four instruments are no longer within our realm," the Queen said.

Aoide didn't know what to say. "How is that possible? I thought they must have been stolen by goblins, or perhaps other musicians..."

"Their magic has departed from Faerie," the Queen said.

Now Aoide grew nervous. They hadn't brought her here to return the instruments, but to punish her.

"As you surely know," the Queen continued, "Allowing magic to pass out of Faerie—either on purpose, or by negligence—violates the Supreme Law. This can be punished by death."

Aoide tried to look calm, but she was shaking with panic. What would they do to her? She would have to beg for mercy.

"My Queen," Aoide said, falling to her hands and knees. "I do not know how this could have happened. I have not gone near the doors to the man-world."

"Yet your instruments must have left through such doors," the Queen said.

"Your Majesty, I am sorry. I do not understand--"

"Magic, leaking out into the man-world," the Queen said, glaring down at Aoide. "After we have kept ourselves hidden so well, for so long. They have chased us from that world with their iron. If they bring their iron here, to our world, then where shall we hide?"

Aoide trembled, staring at the hexagon floor tile below her. "I do not know, Your Majesty."

"You and your musical troupe are in violation of the Supreme Law," the Queen said. "Rhodia the Harpist. The faun called Neus, player of songpipes. The ogre Skezg, bearing in mind that ogres have no legal rights under the Queen's Law anyway. The four of you must recover the stolen instruments from the man-world."

Aoide looked up, surprised. At least she wasn't being imprisoned, or put to death. "Yes, Your Majesty. We will do all we can!"

"You will succeed," the Queen said, "Or you will suffer the full penalty. All four of you. Do you understand?"

"Yes, Your Majesty."

"This will be done entirely at your expense, naturally," the Queen said. "I have assigned Icarus to watch over you and make sure you resolve this matter quickly."

Aoide looked at the sapphire-eyed fairy in black armor, and he gave her a very small smile.

"I will do as Your Majesty desires," Aoide said. She tried not let her relief show.

"Then we are understood," the Queen said. "Go and do as I say."

"Yes, Your Majesty."

The old elf rapped the base of his staff on the floor, and sound flooded in again from all over the room.

Icarus took Aoide's arm to escort her away. She walked along with him, but slowly slipped her elbow from his grasp. He would lead her to one of the black-rose chambers, and there they would teleport across the deadly labyrinth surrounding the palace, to the guardhouse where the front gate had been before the Queen walled it in.

Aoide managed to look calm on the outside, but she was terrified. She had no idea what had happened, so she had no idea where to begin. But she would recover what had been stolen from her. Her life, and her friends' lives, depended on it.

Chapter Ten

Jason sat on the bleachers at school, watching the seniors assemble on the football field in their rented caps and gowns. He could see Mitch making practice tosses in the air with his square blue cap. Dred sat near him, looking bored.

"Hi, Jason," Erin's voice said. She was on the row of bleachers behind him, but she stepped down beside him to talk.

"Hi." Jason smiled at her.

"Are you here by yourself?" Erin asked, looking at the empty space beside him.

"Yep."

"Oh." Erin sat down beside him. "So…I didn't see you at prom."

"I didn't go."

"Yeah, it was pretty lame," Erin said. "But my girlfriends, you know, Kennedy and Parker, they were nuts about it. So I had to do the whole dress thing, the whole make-up and hair thing. Zach was nice, got us the limo and everything."

"Did you have a good time?"

"It wasn't what I expected it to be." Erin shrugged. "But that's life, right?"

Jason nodded. If he had gone to prom with Erin, he thought, he would make sure she had the best night of her life.

Jason couldn't say that, though, so he moved to a subject that felt safer.

"Sorry I haven't been at band practice," he said. "My parents are still mad at me for sneaking off for that audition."

"It's okay," Erin said. "The band's breaking up, anyway."

"Really?" Jason hadn't heard anything about that.

"We kind of have to, don't we?" Erin asked. "Dred's been saying she'll move to the Cities after graduation. And Mitch is going off to Stout for college, in a few months. So that's pretty much it."

"But we can still play together," Jason said.

"I don't think that's very realistic, with everybody moving away."

"I mean you and me. We could still hang out and play. Maybe get another band going. We're both still stuck at this school another year, right?"

"True. That could be fun."

Jason wanted to keep talking to her—about anything, really—but he wasn't sure what to say. She still tied his tongue in knots. He noticed he was crumpling and uncrumpling the paper graduation program in his hand, and he made himself stop.

"There's something I haven't told anybody," Jason said. "I thought it could make a big difference for the band...but then I thought it was kind of a stupid idea."

"What is it?" Erin asked.

"That's pretty hard to explain. If you can come by my house, I'll show you."

"Tell me what it is."

"Yeah, it's not going to make any sense if I just tell you. Want to come by Monday? My parents will be gone, so it'll just be me and Katie."

"And then you can show me this amazing thing that you can't possibly give me a clue about?"

"Yep."

Erin smiled and looked at him for a long moment. "Okay, Jason Becker. I'll come to your house on Monday."

Jason wondered if she thought he was just inviting her over to try and make out with her. He didn't want to give her the wrong idea...but then again, she'd already agreed. He felt scared and elated at the same time.

Then the principal began to speak, and Erin turned to watch. Jason looked at the side of her face for a few seconds more, and then he started to watch the graduation ceremony.

Chapter Eleven

By Monday morning, he was a nervous wreck. As soon as his parents left, he was in his room, trying on different shirts, checking his hair.

"Whatcha doing?" Katie wandered in and plopped on his bed. She was holding an orange plush Tyrannosaurus Rex.

"Nothing, Katie."

"Want to play dinosaurs?"

"I'm busy."

"You said you weren't doing anything!"

"I'm having a friend come over for a while."

"Mom and Dad say you're not allowed," Katie said. "I'm s'posed to call them if you go anywhere. Or if somebody comes over."

"They've got you spying for them, huh?"

"Yep."

"Please don't tell, Katie."

"Who's coming over?"

"My friend, Erin."

"Boy Aaron or girl Erin?"

"Girl Erin."

"Oooh...Is she your girlfriend?"

"No, Katie. And she's probably not even coming."

"You said she was! Make up your mind."

"I mean, she probably forgot, or changed her mind," Jason said.

It was hard for him to believe that Erin Kavanagh was actually coming to hang out with him. He'd never spent any time with her besides band practice and failed auditions.

"Why would she forget?" Katie asked.

"Because she doesn't care that much about me. She has a boyfriend."

"Is he coming, too?"

"He better not be!" Jason was suddenly worried at the idea that Erin would bring Zach and he'd be stuck watching the two of them together the whole time.

Jason took out his cologne, which he'd never taken out of the box since his aunt sent it to him for Christmas. It smelled a little bit like leather and wood, nothing too froofy. He slapped it all over his face with both hands, since he'd once seen a character in a movie apply it that way.

"Why you wearing perfume?" Katie asked.

"It's called 'cologne' when a boy wears it."

"Why you wearing boy perfume?"

"I'm just trying it out."

"Are you in love with Erin?"

"Katie, just give me a break!" Jason shouted. "Stop being a little pest!"

Katie's face crumpled and turned red, and she looked like she was about to cry.

"Play stupid dinosaurs by yourself!" she shouted back. She threw the stuffed T. Rex on his floor and stomped out of the room.

"Katie, sorry, I didn't mean to yell," Jason said, remembering that he needed Katie to keep quiet and not tell their parents about Erin visiting. He followed Katie to her room. After much begging and apologizing, he agreed to make up for yelling by playing Mario Kart on the Wii with her.

The video game actually calmed him down by giving him something to concentrate on, besides the question of whether Erin was actually coming, and the question of whether he'd be able to talk like a somewhat intelligent human being when she was around.

Jason was completely absorbed in being Yoshi, driving his go-kart on the beach, when the doorbell rang.

"I'll get it!" Katie dropped her steering-wheel controller, letting Toad crash into a rocky cliff. She ran out of the living room.

"Wait, Katie!" Jason chased after her. She was already opening the front door.

Erin stood outside the storm door. She waved when she saw Jason, and his heart skipped a beat or three.

Katie pushed open the storm door.

"Are you Erin?" Katie asked.

"I am. Who are you?" Erin smiled.

"That's Katie, my sister." Jason reached over Katie's head and held the door open while Erin stepped inside. Erin hugged an arm around his waist.

"Are you in love with my brother?" Katie asked.

"Katie, don't you want to go play video games? Or watch TV?" Jason asked.

"No, I want to see what you guys are doing," Katie said.

"Katie, we need to talk alone for a minute," Jason said.

"Then I'll tell Mom you had a *girl* come over!"

Jason sighed. Katie really had him trapped on that one.

"Okay, Katie," Jason said. "But you can't tell Mom and Dad what I'm about to show you."

"Is it a secret?" Katie whispered, with her hands over her mouth.

"Yep, it's a big secret."

"I like secrets," Erin said. She winked, and Jason thought he might melt.

"It's out in the garage." Jason led them down the steps to the living room, and from there into the garage.

"Are we going to play?" Erin took out her harmonica.

"Maybe." Jason knelt by his dad's old Corvette and slid out a cardboard box covered with a drop cloth. He'd moved the instruments into it when they shrank to toy size.

Now he removed the drop cloth. Erin and Katie leaned forward to look at the little instruments, all of them carved with fairy runes: the lute with the amethysts in the soundboard, the reed pipes, the silver harp, the drum.

"Oooh, pretty!" Katie said.

"What are these for?" Erin asked.

Jason took a deep breath. "Okay. So the other night, this...goblin sneaks into my house."

"Goblin?" Erin raised an eyebrow.

"It's true!" Katie said. "He was a ugly green monster!"

"Oh...a *goblin*," Erin said, as if this were just a game for Katie's benefit, and she was playing along. "I bet that *was* scary."

"But Jason runned him off!" Katie added.

"Yeah..." Jason actually felt a little relieved Katie was here to back up his story. "So I chased the goblin over to Mrs. Dullahan's house. You know Mrs. Dullahan?"

"I know of her," Erin said. "With the creepy house on the edge of town?"

"She's a witch!" Katie said.

"So, I chase the goblin there, and then...I follow him into the fairy world."

"I like fairies!" Katie contributed.

"And I found these instruments," Jason said. "They're magic."

Erin looked from Jason to Katie, as if trying to figure out the joke.

Jason picked up the lute. "The problem is, they shrank when I brought them back. Just like the goblin—he was smaller when he was here, but he was taller in the fairy world. Still pretty short, though. Everyone over there was short, except for the ogres."

"Of course...the ogres." Erin looked puzzled. And a little worried. She crossed her arms tight and leaned back, away from him.

"Yeah, I know it sounds crazy," Jason said. "But these things make amazing music. Just listen to this, okay?"

Erin stared at him, frowning.

"This isn't really funny, Jason," she said.

"You'll see what I mean. Trust me." Jason touched his guitar pick to one string of the lute, took a deep breath, then plucked it and let it hum. A deep, melancholy sound filled the garage, and he suddenly felt very sad.

He plucked the next string, a higher note, and now he felt wistful, nostalgic, thinking of the time his team had won the county Little League championship. And his fifth birthday party. And his Grandmother baking sugar cookies on Christmas Eve.

Erin frowned and looked away. "That's really powerful," she said, and she sounded a little sad, too.

He plucked the next string, and as it vibrated its slightly higher tone, he felt lonely.

"I wish we had a dog," Katie said. "I would hug him all the time."

The fourth string cheered everybody up. He was glad to be here, with Erin and even his pesky little sister. The girls smiled a little.

The fifth string made everyone laugh and brought fresh, happy energy into the room. The sixth put a huge, blissful smile on everyone's face.

"I like that one best," Katie said.

"It's like each one makes you feel something different," Erin said. "Three kinds of sadness, three kinds of happiness."

"And when you play them all together..." Jason strummed the pick across all six strings.

Erin closed her eyes as the music passed through her. "Oh...*wow*. That's really beautiful."

"Play it some more, Jason!" Katie demanded. "I want more!"

"That's what we like to hear from the audience," Erin said. She smiled at Jason.

"Want to try a whole song?" Jason asked.

"Sure." Erin took out her harmonica.

"You should try this." Jason handed her the matchbook-sized set of reed pipes. "You play it like a harmonica."

"Pan pipes," Erin said. "That's neat. But they're too small to play." Erin held them to her lips. "I'd just blow all the pipes at once." She set it aside and put her harmonica to her lips. "I'll stick with old reliable Monica here."

"What should we play?" Jason set the small lute face-up on his lap.

"I'd really like to hear how 'Remember' sounds on that lute," Erin said. "Think you can handle it?"

"I think so." Jason began playing Erin's song 'Remember' on the lute strings. He used the same hand positions and strings he would have used if he were playing his guitar. The music came out deep, rich and heartbreaking. The lute grew warm in his hands.

Erin followed along with her harmonica for a few bars, then she sang:

Remember the day when you were young,
Remember the time when you believed,
Remember the world where you were loved,
Remember the years when you felt free...

The guitar squirmed like a live animal in Jason's hands. The bent neck straightened out, and the whole lute swelled larger.

"Whoa, what's happening?" Jason asked. "Are you seeing this?"

"That's not possible, is it?" Erin poked at the lute. "It looks like it's *alive* or something."

"It's magic!" Katie said.

"Let's keep playing," Erin said. "I want to see what happens."

They played all the way through 'Remember,' while the lute grew and shifted in his hands. The enchanted instrument brought an incredible power to the song, and all three of them were in tears by the time Erin sang the last verse:

Remember the promise you never kept,
Nothing you said was ever true.
I know you've forgotten all about me,
But I'll never forget about you.

Jason couldn't stop crying. It felt like the song had ripped him open. Katie was blubbering loudly, while Erin held her hands over her face and shuddered.

"Hey, it's okay," Jason whispered. He patted Katie's head with one hand. "Erin? That was really good. You write amazing songs."

Erin kept sobbing into her hands.

"Are you okay?" Jason asked.

Erin slowly lowered her hands, revealing a face that was red and streaked with tears. "I'm sorry. I didn't mean to cry."

"Everybody is," Jason said.

"You know why I was such a spaz about that necklace?" Erin asked. "That was the last birthday present my dad gave me. When I was nine. He left like a month later. Now it's a five-dollar bill in my birthday card, if he remembers at all. And he usually doesn't."

"I'm sorry." Jason took her hand. "Is that what the song is about? Your parents' divorce?"

"It's stupid." Erin pulled her hand away from him and pushed blond and green hair back from her face. "Stupid song."

"It's not," Jason said.

"Can you play something happy now?" Katie asked.

Erin laughed and wiped her eyes. "That's a good idea, Katie. Let's play my happiest song."

"'Stolen Rhino'?" Jason asked.

Erin smiled and blew a few jazzy, upbeat sounds on her harmonica.

"Wait," Jason said. He picked up the little pan pipes and held them out to her. "Play this."

"It's too little."

"It might not stay that way." Jason thumped the instrument in his lap, and Erin gaped.

The lute had transformed into a guitar. Not only was it full-sized, but it fit perfectly in Jason's arms, as if it had been custom-built for him. The fairy runes were carved all over the guitar, giving it a strange, engraved texture under his fingers. The little amethysts were still embedded here and there in the soundboard, but they hadn't changed size at all, so they looked tiny.

"That's amazing," Erin said. She took the little pan pipes from his hand and studied them. "Where did you get these instruments, again?"

"It's just what I said," Jason told her. "There's a door to the fairy world in Mrs. Dullahan's yard. That's where I found them."

"I want to go to the fairy world!" Katie said.

"It's very dangerous over there," Jason said. "And crazy. I'm not going back."

"But I want to," she complained.

"You really don't," Jason said. Now he felt like an idiot for talking about fairies in front of his little sister—of course she'd be interested. "They aren't nice fairies like in stories. They carry big swords and they walk around threatening everyone. They're nasty, scary fairies. You have to stay away, Katie."

"Scary fairies?" Katie pouted. Her eyes were still puffy from crying.

"Scary fairies," Jason repeated, nodding.

Erin held the tiny pipes to her lips and blew. The sound was haunting, and a cool breeze seemed to pass through the garage, though the doors to the outside were closed.

The pipes swelled in her hands as if she were blowing up a row of balloons. Then the instrument was large enough for her to play each pipe individually. As with the lute-turned-guitar, each pipe gave a different sound and inspired a different, overpowering emotion. As Erin blew on the pipes, Jason felt like his brain was working faster, generating lots of ideas. He was getting excited.

"Are you ready to play yet?" Katie asked.

"I'm ready," Erin said, giving Jason a smile. She blew some bright notes through the more cheerful-toned pipes. "I'm not too sure how to play this thing."

"Just treat it like it's your harmonica," Jason said. "I think it adapts to you."

"Cool!" Erin played more notes, and the pan pipes wiggled to fit better into her fingers. Erin laughed. "It tickles."

Jason began playing "Stolen Rhino" on his guitar. It was a fast, peppy, simple song.

Erin accompanied him on the pipes. The guitar vibrated in his hands, tuning into the pipe sound and harmonizing with it. Hot wind tousled his hair, but he couldn't tell where it was coming from.

Erin lowered the pipes and sang:

You took me for a date at the zoo
Said my love left something to prove
So I did all I knew to do
I stole a fat rhinoceros for you!

Stolen rhino, in my car
Stolen rhino, now love me more
Stolen rhino, I did it for you
Stolen rhino, don't make me steal two!

Katie was laughing her head off. Erin played a musical interlude. The pan pipes shifted and molted in her fingers, and finally settled into the shape of a wooden harmonica carved with fairy runes.

After the fun song, the whole room seemed to glow, as if everyone and everything were infused with a warm, golden light.

"I love that song!" Katie shouted. "Play it again now!"

Jason and Erin's eyes met, and they both burst into uncontrollable giggles, and then full-blown hysterical laughter, as if they'd both had nitrous oxide at the dentist's office. It was a few minutes before they could calm down enough to talk again.

"Wow," Erin said. She looked at her new harmonica, Jason's guitar, and the little drum and harp still in the box. "Wow, wow, wow. I'm starting to believe you really got these from fairies."

"I wasn't kidding."

"We have to call Mitch and Dred!" Erin said. "Like, tonight. We have to get together and jam with these new instruments and see what they can do."

"I want to come!" Katie said.

"I can't go anywhere tonight," Jason said. "I'm grounded, plus I have to work at my new job. My dad could check to make sure I'm there. He does that."

"Where are you working?" Erin asked.

Jason looked down at the floor. "Buddy McSlawburger's."

"You're working at Bloody McSlobberbooger's?" Erin laughed. "Do you wear the funny hat?"

"Everyone has to wear the funny hat."

"We have to do this soon," Erin said. "I'm dying to see Mitch and Dred's faces when they see this."

"Then it'll have to be during the day when my parents are gone," Jason said.

"I wanna come, too!" Katie said.

"And it'll have to be a day I'm not babysitting Katie."

"I'm not a *baby*."

"Okay," Erin said. "Let's call them and figure out a time. I'm so excited, Jason!"

Erin hugged his neck tight, and Jason wished he wasn't sitting in a chair, and that there wasn't a guitar between them.

Chapter Twelve

In Mitch's garage, Mitch sat at his keyboard and Dred sat behind her drum kit. They stared as if Jason and Erin had lost their minds. It was Thursday afternoon, the first time all four of them could get together.

"I'm serious," Erin said, holding up her new, rune-engraved harmonica. "Magic instruments."

"Right," Dred said.

"There are two more." Jason took the two remaining toy-sized instruments out of the cardboard box he'd brought over. "Dred, obviously you get the drum. So that leaves you with the harp, Mitch." He gave Mitch the little silver harp, and Mitch just looked at it, puzzled.

"How am I supposed to play this thing?" Mitch asked.

"You'll see." Jason held out the muffin-sized drum to Dred, who just stared at it like it was a dead fish. He set it down on her snare drum.

"This is really sad, you guys," Dred said. "How can you both go completely insane on the same day?"

"Let's just play a little," Erin said. "Watch."

Erin started the tune to "First Road Out of Here" on her harmonica. A cool breeze passed through the hot garage, stirring some magazines stacked next to Mitch's keyboard. The Claudia Lafayette poster on the wall billowed out at the bottom, since it was secured only by thumbtacks at the top.

Dred and Mitch looked at each other while the gentle breeze tossed their hair.

Jason joined in, and the breeze became hotter. The guitar was warm.

The little wind stopped when Erin lowered the harmonica to sing the lyrics. The song conjured intense feelings in Jason, a combination of loneliness and wanderlust and a touch of nostalgia, a stronger reaction than he'd ever had to it before.

"Those are amazing," Mitch said, when Erin stopped singing for a harmonica interlude in the middle of the song. Mitch strummed the little harp with his fingertip. "Great sound, but how do I play it?"

"Turn it on its side," Jason said. "Pretend it's the strings of a piano."

"It won't work that way," Mitch said.

"It will in a minute."

Mitch rolled his eyes and turned the harp on its side. He tapped at the strings, as if his fingertips were the hammers inside a piano. The harp expanded and reshaped itself, growing more strings in between the existing ones. A keyboard grew out of the side facing Mitch, the black keys made of onyx, the white made of opal.

"Whoa!" Mitch stood up and backed away. "That's all kinds of messed up. What's happening?"

"It's adapting to you," Jason said. "You have to keep playing so it'll finish changing."

"Changing into what?"

"Whatever works best for you."

Mitch played the keys, and the strings vibrated as he did it, though there weren't any hammers tapping them. A gleaming silver lid unfolded from one edge of the harp and closed over the strings. Buttons made of gemstones blossomed across the top, imitating his synthesizer keyboard.

Mitch shook his head, but he kept playing. The keyboard's sound was deep and rich.

Dred just gaped. She hadn't touched the little drum Jason had given her.

They reached the end of the song.

"This must be some kind of weird dream," Mitch said. "I'm dreaming, right? This can't happen."

"Let's do another song," Erin said.

"How about 'Nuclear Morning'?" Mitch suggested. "I want to hear how that sounds on these things."

Erin started with the harmonica part, and Jason and Mitch joined in. Dred sat back, arms folded, shaking her head.

The keyboard sprouted silver wires that snaked around and plugged into Mitch's other keyboards, as well as the small laptop he kept connected to increase his range of sample and sound options. The old keyboard and the laptop turned silver, and the fairy runes etched themselves all over the surface of them, as if the magical instrument was infecting them like a virus.

"Whoa, whoa!" Mitch backed away again. "That is crazy." Jason and Erin stopped playing.

"Keep playing!" a voice yelled.

The elementary school kids from Mitch's neighborhood who sometimes watched them practice, two boys and a girl, were standing in the driveway. All three were watching the band intently.

"Mitch, the audience demands more," Erin said with a grin. "Are you ready?"

Mitch looked at Dred, who still had her arms folded. "Dred?"

"I think you're right, Mitch," Dred said. "I'm the one having a crazy dream. I'm just going to sit here until I wake up."

"It's not a dream," Jason said. "These were made by fairies—"

"No, no, I heard the story," Dred said. "It's nonsense. This is all just...nonsense."

"Play some more!" another kid demanded. A fourth kid, one Jason hadn't seen before, who had just arrived on a skateboard.

"Something for the skater kid," Erin said. "Which song do you think, Mitch?"

Mitch looked between Erin and the kids. "Um...Cinderella Night? Fast?"

"Fast," Jason agreed.

They played, and the kids danced to rapid tempo, though Dred still hadn't joined in on her drums. During the song, more kids showed up dancing in the driveway and the front yard, including middle and high schoolers, as if the music had drawn them all out of their homes and down the street. It was turning into a semi-outdoor concert.

With three of the fairy instruments going, the guitar in Jason's hands really started to buzz and cast off heat. Fortunately, the keyboard seemed to turn the hot wind circulating inside the garage into something wet and cooling, like the breeze off Lake Wisota.

Energized by the growing audience, and unregulated by any drummer, Jason, Erin and Mitch kept accelerating the song, playing an extended instrumental version of it. The dancers moved faster with them, colliding with each other and laughing. One of the girls in the audience waved her iPhone around, capturing images of the band and the dancing crowd.

Mitch went wild on the keyboards as he grew familiar with his new instrument. Erin and Jason stepped back and let him have an extended solo. He played as if possessed, his tongue sticking out of his mouth, his hands a blur across the keys, the assorted gemstones on the keyboard case glowing brighter and brighter.

Jason watched the crowd, amazed at how they'd come from nowhere.

Erin nudged Jason, and he looked back at Mitch. Blue steam erupted from the gemstones, forming into a cloud around Mitch, but Mitch either didn't notice or didn't care.

The cloud grew larger and drifted through the garage, passing over Jason and Erin. It was cool and refreshing, not hot. No wonder Mitch didn't mind.

It drifted out, with a trail of cool blue steam still feeding into it from the keyboard. The cloud expanded as Mitch's solo continued, and it rose above the crowd.

Mitch hit a crescendo and leaned back, dropping his hands in his lap. He was drenched in sweat and gasping for air.

The cloud rumbled, and then dumped rain all over the dancing kids.

The audience shrieked and scattered, all of them dripping wet and laughing. Jason watched them spread out through the neighborhood, jostling each other as they ran.

"Did that really just happen?" Erin asked.

"Which part?" Jason asked her.

"Any of it. That was unreal."

"Oh, man," Mitch said, wiping his face with his T-shirt. "I *love* this keyboard."

"This is too crazy for me," Dred stood up, tossing her keys in the air. She left the little fairy drum where Jason had placed it, on top of her snare. "I'm going for a milkshake. Anybody coming?"

"Why don't you stay and try out your drum?" Erin asked.

"It's not my drum," Dred said. "And I don't believe in magic."

They watched Dred climb into her van and drive away.

"Man...I *love* this keyboard," Mitch repeated. He was staring at it with a crazy grin.

Chapter Thirteen

Aoide flew over the bright green Poisoned Forest, far south of Sidhe City. She'd been flying all day, from dawn until nearly dusk, and every muscle in her back ached. Fortunately, she'd just caught a hot south-moving breeze, and now she could spread out her wings and drift for a while. Rhodia floated alongside Aoide, her long pink hair twisting in the wind, her face looking tired and miserable. Aoide felt the same way.

The dark waters of the Acheron River flowed wide and sluggish through the forest below. The forest itself was known for its impenetrable tangles of plants with sharp spines and deadly venom. It was also home to carnivorous plants that camouflaged themselves in the jungle foliage until a jumping deer or a duck-billed bear stepped within snapping distance.

The Poisoned Forest was too dangerous to cross on foot or on beastback, so they flew. Neus the faun and Skezg the ogre couldn't fly, so they hadn't come along. Lucky guys.

Icarus of the Queensguard flew ahead of them, leading them southward along the great river. He'd roused Aoide and Rhodia from sleep before dawn to make this journey. He didn't seem tired at all, despite his heavy black armor. The armor must have been enchanted to make it feel weightless, Aoide thought. He occasionally glanced back with an annoyed look, as if he felt the two musicians were flying too slowly.

"Are we there yet?" Rhodia gasped.

"I hope so," Aoide replied.

Below them, the Acheron River grew wider and shallower, eventually spreading out into a dark marsh that stretched from horizon to horizon, full of swampy little islands. Stalk-shaped plants, giant sugarcanes, grew from the swamp, some of them taller and thicker than city watchtowers. Their foliage overlapped, concealing most of the ground beneath them.

Aoide sighed in relief when Icarus began to spiral down from the sky towards the swamp. Aoide and Rhodia followed.

He landed on a small, marshy island, where Aoide and Rhodia's bare feet splashed into the wet mud. Icarus's black boots sank even farther. The thick towers of cane overshadowed them, and they were walled in by dense stands of smaller canes, which were still four times taller than Aoide.

The entire swamp smelled sweet, as if they'd landed in a confectioner's shop. The humid, syrupy air was dense with flying insects.

"This place is so gross," Rhodia said. She lifted one foot, which was covered in gloppy, sticky mud.

An insect landed on Aoide's arm and pressed its big, trumpet-shaped snout against her skin. It began to suck, and the sensation was painful. She slapped it away, but its mouth left a coin-sized circle of itchy red on her arm.

Overhead, a fuzzy creature the size of a small dog with huge, leathery wings swooped down at Aoide with its mouth open. She and Rhodia screamed and ducked, while Icarus backed away, drawing his bright iron sword.

The creature ate a swath through the flying bugs, leaving a streak of empty air behind it. It tilted upwards and flew high along the trunk of a giant old cane. It grabbed onto the thick leaves on the cane's side and hung upside down, chewing its mouthful of bugs.

"What was that?" Aoide asked.

"A sugar bat," Icarus said. "The sugar cane makes the swamp water sweet, and the sugar water attracts all these swarms of bugs. So the bats grow very fat here."

"Ugh," Rhodia said, waving away more of the trumpet-mouthed suckerflies. "I can't believe we had to come all the way to the sugar swamps. I'm ready for a nice bed and a tea-and-pastry."

"You won't find those here," Icarus said. He swung his long

sword at a wall of sugarcane, felling a dozen of the plants. Then he stepped forward and swung the sword again, hacking a path through the dense growth. "Come on."

Aoide and Rhodia followed at distance, leery of his sword. Iron was deadly to fairies, which was why the Queensguard used iron weapons.

The mud slurped at their feet with every step, and they swatted flies from their faces and arms as they walked along the path of chopped sugarcane. High, dense staffs of cane surrounding them on both sides.

"We are *literally* in the sticks," Rhodia complained.

"Watch out for the swamp bugs," Icarus called back. "They'll suck the sweetness right out of you."

"I don't have much sweetness left," Rhodia said.

They hopped over a creek of dark sugar water onto the next marshy island, which was also dense with cane. Icarus held up a hand for them to stop, and then untied a spiral-shaped goat horn from his belt. He blew a long note to announce their arrival.

"Who blows there?" a deep, gristly voice asked through the screen of sugarcane.

"I am Icarus, a captain of the Queensguard," Icarus said. "With me are Aoide the Lutist and Rhodia the Harpist."

"Fairies!" the voice sneered. There was a sound like hacking, and then spitting. "Go away."

"We've come on the orders of the Queen," Icarus said.

"*Your* Queen," the gristly voice said. "We are queenless here."

"All of Faerie is the domain of Queen Mab," Icarus said.

"Not this patch of swamp," the voice replied.

"We've come to hire your services," Icarus said. "The Queen offers a generous payment."

"I don't take fairy gold," the voice said. "It has a way of turning to broom flowers in a day or two."

"We have brought many forms of payment," Icarus said, looking Aoide. Aoide carried in her pouch an assortment of jewels and silver coins, all of her savings, as well as the savings of Rhodia, Neus, and Skezg. The Queen was making them pay the hunter's fee.

"Then come around," the voice said. "There's a break in the cane off to your left."

Icarus sheathed his sword. The three fairies followed the wall of cane around the curve of the marshy island and found the opening.

Aoide and Rhodia shared worried looks as they followed Icarus through.

At the highest point in the island sat a hut made of sugarcane, brambles and mud. A garden of beets grew beside it.

Next to the hut was a sugarcane the size of a tree. An elf with graying beard stubble and a tattered old gardening hat sat back against it, chewing a juicy splinter of cane, his horsehair clothes and sandals caked in dried mud. The elf eyed them suspiciously.

"Thank you for the invitation," Icarus said. "We would like to hire you as a tracker and hunter. Four objects of high magic must be found."

"And you fancy city fairies came all the way here, just to ask a simple country elf for help." The elf smirked.

"But you aren't just a simple country elf," Icarus said. "The scrolls say you were a highly decorated knight in the Great Elf and Fairy War."

"A war your side won," the elf said. "It wasn't so 'Great' for our side." The elf spat.

"That was thousands of years ago," Icarus said.

"Doesn't seem so long ago." The elf sneered at Aoide and Rhodia. "The whole realm used to be known as Aelfer, or the Elflands. I bet you young brats didn't even know that."

"I'm not a young brat," Aoide said. "I'm nearly seven centuries old. And Rhodia just had her five hundredth birthday."

"And I've lived ten thousand years longer than you children!" the elf barked. "Show some respect for your elders."

"The Queen requires your service," Icarus repeated.

"Now, hold your quarterhorses there, city fairy." The elf stood, leaning on a thick staff of sugarcane. He looked at the golden seal of the Queen on Icarus's breastplate, and then pointed at Aoide and Rhodia. "I know what you are, warrior, but who are these two?"

"As I said, Aoide the Lutist and Rhodia the Harpist. Musicians."

"You've brought musicians?" the elf asked. He raised his hat in greeting, revealing long and stringy hair. His left ear was tall and pointy, but his right ear ended in scar tissue, and the tip of it was missing. "Ladies, welcome to my back corner of the sugar swamps. I am called Hoke the Swamp Elf, unfortunately. A wind of ill luck blew me here long ago."

"Hoke?" Rhodia said. "I've never heard of an elf name like that."

Aoide elbowed her to be quiet.

"If you like, you can call me by my given name, Hokealussiplatytorpinquarnartnuppy Melaerasmussanatolinkarrutorpicus Darnathiopockettlenocbiliotroporiqqua Bellefrost. But most people call me 'Hoke.'" He chewed on his sugarcane splinter. "So, you brought musicians to entertain me. Why don't you play a song for us?"

"That's just the problem," Aoide said. "Someone stole our instruments."

"And so the purpose of our visit--" Icarus began.

"I would think musicians could improvise," Hoke said. "Can't you sing or nothing? There's not much music to be had, way out here. No taverns, no amphitheater. Nobody to talk to, really."

"I would like to discuss the terms of our bargain--" Icarus tried again.

"First, I want my song," Hoke said. "Then I'll hear whatever it is you want to say."

Aoide and Rhodia looked at each other. Rhodia cleared her throat.

"*Mi mi mi mi miiiii...*" Rhodia sang, warming up.

Aoide sang the first line of the song, and then Rhodia joined in. It was "Sometimes in the Night," a ballad about an elf and a fairy who fell in love during the Great War, and had to keep their love a secret. It began as a sweet and romantic song, and ended tragically.

As Aoide and Rhodia sang the last verse, Aoide thought she could see a little wetness in Hoke's eyes. He wiped them with the back of his muddy hand and looked away.

"I do miss being young," Hoke said. "Young and foolish and ready to love."

Aoide and Rhodia smiled and curtsied, as if he'd applauded.

Hoke looked at Icarus and sighed.

"What is this help that you and Mad Queen Mab want from me?" Hoke asked.

"You will not refer to Her Majesty that way! It is forbidden!" Icarus snapped. His black-gloved hand flew to the handle of his sheathed sword.

"She's the one crushed the whole realm under her iron boot."

"Treason!" Icarus said.

"Relax, Icarus," Aoide said. "He's ready to listen now. Right, Hoke?"

"I will listen, but no promises," Hoke said. "I am very busy here."

Rhodia looked around the swamp with a puzzled expression, probably wondering what could keep him busy in this dismal place.

"Go ahead, Icarus," Aoide said.

"As I have been attempting to say," Icarus said, "Four instruments of high magic have been stolen."

"And I can guess it from there," Hoke said. "You want me and my cornhorses to track them down."

"What's a cornhorse?" Rhodia asked.

"Some call 'em unicorns, I call 'em cornhorses," Hoke said. "Best creature for sniffing out magic, except for a banshee wolf, and good luck finding one of those for hire."

"So, where are the unicorns?" Rhodia asked.

"Unicorn's a shy critter," Hoke said. "Everybody get down low, on your knees, so you don't look so darn big."

Aoide and Rhodia lifted their skirts and squatted on their heels in the mud. They looked around the thick stands of cane, eager to see a live unicorn. Aoide had only seen them in sculpture or paintings. They were very rare, very skittish.

"You, too," Hoke said to Icarus.

"A Queensguard will not kneel to an elf," Icarus said.

"You aren't kneeling *to* me, wasp-brain," Hoke said. "You want these cornhorses to come or not?"

"Just sit down already," Aoide whispered.

Icarus scowled at her. He spread an embroidered silk handkerchief on a muddy log of fallen sugarcane before sitting down on it. He kept his hand on his belt, near his sword.

Hoke squatted and lay his sugarcane staff on its side in the mud. He hummed a high note.

"Cinnamon!" Hoke sang out. "Berrymuffin! Buttercake! Come on, girls!"

There was a tiny splashing sound behind a thick patch of sugarcane. The first unicorn nosed her way out, timidly, tiptoeing on her cloven hooves. She was smaller than a pygmy pony, with a reddish coat. Her tail and mane, and the spiral horn that spiked out from the center of her forehead, were the color of dark cinnamon.

She took a few steps forward on trembling legs, then stopped, staring at the fairies.

"She's just a little scared," Hoke whispered.

"Awww," Rhodia whispered. "It's okay, little girl."

The second unicorn emerged just as cautiously. Her coat was the color of brown sugar, her mane and horn a strawberry shade of red, her eyes like big blueberries. She stood close to the first unicorn, their sides nearly touching.

"Buttercake!" Hoke called again.

The third unicorn walked out meekly, with her nose lowered until it almost dragged the swampy earth. Her coat was the color of yellow cake, and her mane and horn were like pink frosting. Buttercake stayed behind the first two unicorns, gazing at Aoide with huge chocolate-colored eyes.

"Hi, Buttercake," Aoide whispered, smiling.

"Don't speak to my cornhorses!" Hoke snapped.

"Are we ready to give them the scent?" Icarus asked.

"Not so fast, city fairy," Hoke said. "First I see my payment."

Icarus nodded at Aoide.

Aoide sighed and lifted the drawstring pouch. She was determined to keep as much of her friends' savings as she could.

She chose a big ruby, one of her own jewels, and held it out to Hoke. "Will this do as a first payment?"

The elf yawned.

Aoide took out a pearl, also her own, and laid it next to the ruby in her palm. "This?"

Hoke crossed his arms and looked away.

"You don't have to use all your own things to pay him," Rhodia said. "Throw in that emerald Neus gave you."

Aoide added the emerald to her palm.

The elf squinted one eye and leaned close to Aoide's hand, then snatched the gemstones away. They disappeared from his hand—he must have slipped them into a pocket somewhere in his mud-caked clothes.

"And twice as much when the task is done," Hoke said.

"We can do that," Icarus said.

Aoide bit her lip. It was going to cost nearly everything, leaving the four musicians broke. They had no choice, though.

"Now, we'll need the scent," Hoke said. He pointed at Aoide. "You. Come and stand by me. Don't move too fast, or you'll spook off the cornhorses."

She did as the elf said, stepping lightly and carefully.

"Buttercake," Hoke whispered. He pulled a beet from the

garden and held it out. "Come here, little girl."

Buttercake advanced slowly towards Hoke, giving Aoide a wide berth and a spooked look. Buttercake nibbled the beet in Hoke's hand, and the elf petted her mane.

"There," Hoke said. "Now, we need to find these missing instruments, Buttercake. Have a sniff."

His calloused hand seized Aoide's and put it close to the unicorn's mouth. Buttercake sniffed Aoide's palm, then swished her pink tail.

"What kind of instruments am I looking for, exactly?" Hoke asked.

"I play a lute," Aoide said. "Rhodia has a silver harp. And there's pan pipes and a drum. But the instruments can change depending on who plays them. If a fairy blew on Neus' pan pipes, they might turn into a flute."

"So what do they look like now?" Hoke asked.

"It depends who took them," Aoide said.

"You don't have any idea who it was?" Hoke asked.

"Nor do we know their intentions," Icarus said. "The Queen's seer tells us they have left the realm of Faerie. These instruments could cause incredible destruction in the human world. In the hands of anyone not properly trained by the Musicians' Guild..."

"It could be a nightmare," Aoide said.

"The man-world." Hoke lifted his hat and scratched around in his stringy, dirty hair. "Haven't been there in a century or ten. So, we don't know what the things look like or who has 'em or why. They'll take some time to track down. Buttercake's my best sniffer, though. Next fairy!"

Aoide backed off and let Buttercake sniff Rhodia's hand. Rhodia giggled and tried to pet the unicorn, but the little creature skittered back out of reach.

"Hands off my cornhorse!" Hoke barked. "And where's the scents for the other two instruments?"

"Here." Aoide opened another pouch. It contained a swatch of Skezg's filthy shirt, to give the unicorn the ogre's smell. It also had a locket of Neus' white fur, since he didn't wear clothes. The faun let the shaggy goat fur on his hips and legs serve as trousers. He didn't even wear shoes, because the bottoms of his stubby feet and toes were coated with hard hoof.

Buttercake sniffed inside the pouch for a couple of minutes.

Then she stuck out her tongue and backed away.

"What about the other unicorns?" Icarus asked. Cinnamon and Berrymuffin had wandered away a little bit, to slurp from a pool of sugar water.

"If you think I'm taking more than one unicorn up to man-world, then you're madder than Queen Mab."

"I warned you!" Icarus reached for his sword, but Aoide grabbed his arm and shushed him.

"It's just a figure of speech," Hoke said. He snorted, then spat a ball of bright orange elf-snot into a puddle near Icarus's boot.

Icarus opened his mouth. Aoide was pretty sure that whatever he said next would lead to an argument or a fight, so she cut him off.

"Is that all you need to begin your search?" Aoide asked Hoke.

"Sounds like that's all you have," Hoke said. "Do we at least know through which doorway the thief entered the man-world? Was it Glastonbury Door?"

"We don't know," Aoide said.

Hoke shook his head and lowered the brim of his hat. He resumed sitting under the shade of the leafy sugar cane by his hut. Buttercake nibbled some flowering weeds beside him.

"When do you intend to begin searching?" Icarus asked.

"After we've had time to rest." Hoke pulled the hat down over his eyes. "Buttercake's a delicate one. Needs her beauty sleep."

"This is urgent!" Icarus snarled.

"Then I'd be better get plenty of sleep," Hoke said. "Don't want me slipping up."

"He said he'll do it, Icarus," Aoide said.

"He'd better. Or we'll show him that Her Majesty Queen Mab does, indeed, rule the swamplands!" Icarus stepped away, out through the break in the wall of cane.

"What a sourdrop," Hoke said.

"He's kind of cranky," Aoide said. "We really do appreciate your help. We really, really need our instruments back. Sorry about Mister Whineyboots out there."

"If they can be found, Buttercake will find them," Hoke said from under his hat. Buttercake looked up and blinked at her name, then resumed grazing.

Aoide and Rhodia walked toward the gap in the sugarcane.

"Will this really work?" Rhodia whispered. "Those unicorns look useless."

"They say unicorns are more than what they appear to be," Aoide whispered. She nudged Rhodia's arm and pointed.

Cinnamon raised her head from a sugary pool, grasping a black and red swamp cobra in her mouth. Its hooded head arched above the unicorn's face, and its fiery red eyes glared down at her. The cobra hissed, with its long fangs dripping venom, and poised to strike the unicorn's soft nose.

Cinnamon snapped her head from side to side, whipping the cobra like a rope. Cracking sounds burst all along the snake's spine. When Cinnamon finally stopped shaking, the long cobra lay limp in her mouth. She sucked up the cobra's body like a noodle. When she'd devoured it, she belched, her ears flattening and her mouth flaring wide. Then she trotted off into the swamp.

Chapter Fourteen

Jason decided to stop by The Creamery in the middle of Friday afternoon, well after the lunch rush but before people got off work, so the place would be as quiet as it got. Erin sometimes talked about being bored that time of day, with nothing to do.

As he rode his bike through the streets of the little town, he imagined how it might go. She'd be happy to take a break. They could have an ice cream at one of the little tables outside on the sidewalk (and he'd have a cone of Chocolate Cashew Snowslide, his favorite flavor). He was determined to tell Erin how he felt about her.

Normally, the idea of talking about such things created a tense ball of nerves deep in his gut and stopped his mouth from working properly. The more he played his new guitar, though, the bolder he felt. It made him feel like taking risks.

He'd even brought the song "Angel Sky," again on a folded page of notebook paper in his pocket, though he'd rewritten some of the verses a number of times since his last attempt to present the song to the band. Maybe telling Erin how much he liked her and giving her the song at the same time would be too much, and she would deem him a creepy stalker guy. But having it in his pocket was like a statement to himself that he was going to make things happen today.

He rode along the sidewalk and glanced into the plate-glass front window of The Creamery. Erin was there behind the ice cream counter, in her paper Creamery hat and white apron. She leaned over the counter, talking intently to someone.

He passed the huge ice-cream-cone-shaped chalkboard in the window. On the other side, he could see Erin was talking to Zach, her boyfriend. He took her hand, and Erin smiled, shaking her head about something while she spoke.

All his nerves crashed. It was scary enough trying to talk about his feelings with her. He definitely wasn't going to do it with her current boyfriend right there. It would just turn into a fight with Zach—not exactly the afternoon he'd envisioned.

Jason turned the next corner and rode up the block, so he wouldn't pass The Creamery again. It was a bad idea, anyway. She was already with someone. He had no reason to think she would rather be with him.

A few hours later, Jason stepped up to the counter at Buddy McSlawburger's, facing a long line of customers. The Friday night shift was busy. He saw a number of people he knew from school, and all of them seemed to be pointing at Jason and smiling at each other.

Like every McSlawburger's employee, Jason wore the trademark funny hat. It was like a baseball cap, but with a giant bouncing "slawburger" sewn to the top. The thing was stuffed with cotton and included a bun, burger, cheese and slaw, all made of felt. The top bun tilted jauntily to one side, making the tall fake burger bounce and sway every time you turned your head. There was even a spring inside it to enhance the effect. It looked especially goofy with a group of employees running around behind the counter, the ridiculously tall burgers on their hats swaying and jiggling all over the place.

"Welcome to Buddy McSlawburger's," Jason said to his first customer, a hefty tattooed biker couple. "Would you like a Slawburger Special today?"

"No!" the fat, bearded biker guy said. "I want two of them cheeseburgers, but none of that slaw junk. I hate that stuff. What do you want, baby?"

"A hot dog," the woman said. "*No* slaw. Got that? *No* slaw."

"Two slawburgers with cheese, hold the slaw," Jason said into the microphone. "One slawdog, hold the slaw."

"And I want some fries," the biker guy added. "But none of that canned chili junk on it."

"One chili-cheese fry, hold the chili-cheese," Jason said.

Jason's next customer was his math teacher, Coach Bauer.

"Hey there, kiddo," the Coach said. "Kiddo" was his generic name for any student who didn't participate in sports or cheerleading. "Double cheeseburger. None of the slaw, I hate that stuff."

"Double slawburger with cheese, hold the slaw," Jason said into the mike. It was already turning into a long night.

A group of four sophomores came to his register next, two boys and two girls. They'd been among those pointing and smiling about him. Jason sighed. As if his day weren't bad enough, now he was about to get ridiculed by younger kids.

"Hi, Jason!" one girl said, waving. Jason had no idea what her name was.

"Uh, hi," Jason said. "Welcome to McSlawburger's."

"I told you it was him," one of the guys said.

"You're even cuter than in the video!" the other girl said. The guy next to her scowled a little.

"Video?" Jason asked.

"We watched it like twenty times!" the first girl said. The two girls leaned together, held up their index fingers like microphones, and sang a verse of Erin's "Cinderella Night" in screeching, off-key voices:

Cinderella, Cinderella beware,
Don't give yourself up on a dare...

"Would you budge along?" a crabby-looking older man in a plaid shirt said behind them. "Some of us are trying to order food here."

"What video?" Jason asked.

"I told you it wasn't him," the scowling boy said.

"It is!" the scowling boy's girlfriend said. "You play the guitar, right?"

"Yeah," Jason said. Both the girls squealed. It was so unexpected that he jumped a little. "So, can I take your order?" he asked.

"When are you putting out another video?" the first girl asked.

"Where's your next concert?" the non-scowling boy asked. "We'll totally come."

"I don't know..." Jason said.

"Does your band have a Facebook page?" the boy asked.

"A MySpace?" the second girl asked.

"Not really. How do you know about my band, again?" Jason asked.

"Nobody cares about your band!" barked the man in plaid.

"Sorry, I have to work," Jason said.

"Why are you working *here* when you can play like that?" the first girl asked.

"Hurry it up!" the plaid-jacket man shouted.

"Do you guys just want slawburgers?" Jason asked the four kids.

"No slaw," the first girl said, and the others hurried to agree.

"Four slawburgers, no slaw," Jason said into the microphone.

The second girl grabbed a napkin and wrote on it. "I'm Wendy," she said. "Call me when you're playing somewhere. Or just, you know, if you want to talk. About anything." She handed him the napkin, which had her phone number and email address under the McSlawburger's logo. The boy who was with her scowled even more.

"I'd better give him my phone number, too." The second girl jotted it down on another napkin and handed it to Jason. "Just in case there's a concert," she explained to her boyfriend.

"You can pick up your burgers at the end of the counter," Jason said. He didn't know what to do with the napkins, so he stuffed them in his pocket.

"Bye, Jason!" the two girls said as they walked to the pick-up area. Then they broke down giggling, grabbing each others' arms. The guy who seemed to like Jason waved, too, while the other one kept scowling as he walked away.

Jason took the man in the plaid shirt's order—slawburger, hold the slaw. Then there were more kids from school talking about Jason's "video." Over the next hour or so, Jason collected phone numbers from five girls and two guys, asking to know when the band would play again.

When he finally got his fifteen-minute break, Jason walked back into the kitchen and checked his phone. He had to keep it turned off during work, because the assistant manager, Mona, couldn't tolerate employees using cell phones.

There were several texts from Mitch, insisting that Jason call him right away. One text linked to a YouTube video.

"Hey, Tadd," Jason said to the guy at the french-fry station, who was in his grade.

"Huh?" Tadd looked up from the big can of McSlawburger's Chili Cheese, which he was spooning onto a basket of fries.

"Do you have your laptop here?" Jason asked. He knew Tadd brought it to work to use the fast-food restaurant's free Wi-Fi during his breaks.

"Oh, yeah," Tadd said.

"Mind if I borrow it?"

"Sure thing. Great video, dude. Though next time, I'd recommend a higher quality camera. Maybe a tripod. I'm into handheld as much as the next guy, but that video was swinging all over the place."

"Yeah, some sixth grade kid in Mitch's neighborhood shot it with her phone."

"Kid with a phone. Very raw. Very real. Breaking boundaries. I like it."

"Thanks..." Jason said, and he continued on to the back door.

He sat on the uncomfortable concrete bench out back, and he finally saw the video everyone was talking about.

It was from yesterday, Jason and Erin and Mitch playing "Cinderella Night" at Mitch's house. The viewpoint bounced wildly from the band in the garage, to the kids dancing in the driveway and front yard, the sky, the street, the grass and shrubbery outside Mitch's house. Jason remembered the middle school girl who'd been waving her iPhone around while dancing. She must have uploaded this.

Jason found himself entranced by the music, swaying as he watched.

It showed the whole song, including the blue cloud pouring up from the garage, and everyone screaming and running as the downpour drenched them.

According to YouTube, the video had been watched 90,342 times since it was uploaded the previous night.

"Totally great song, yo," somebody said behind him. The burger fryer, a bearded guy named Steve who was a few years older than him, was leaning over Jason's shoulder. Jason hadn't even realized anyone had come outside.

"Thanks," Jason said.

"Who's the chick? She's totally hot."

"She only dates high school guys," Jason lied.

"Oh, bummer. Tell her I said hi, little dude."

"Right." Jason closed the laptop. He carried it across the

parking lot towards the Dumpster, to get away from Steve. He dialed Mitch.

"Finally!" Mitch said. "Have you seen it?"

"Yeah. How did that happen?"

"Kelly Kaiser, man. Eighth-grader, lives three houses down."

"Everybody seems to like it," Jason said. "Lots of people are asking when we're going to do a show. Too bad we don't have any gigs, right?"

"This is just the beginning, man," Mitch said. "If people like that crummy video with half a song, imagine what they'll say when we put out a *good* video."

"That's not a bad idea," Jason said.

Back at the bench, Steve stood up, stretched and opened the door to go back inside. Mona, the assistant manager, stepped out, smiled at Steve as he passed her, then glared hard at Jason.

"No cell phones!" Mona snapped.

"I'm on break," Jason said.

"Not for long!" Mona crossed her arms, looked at her watch, and then stared at him.

"Man, forget Bloody McSlobberbooger's," Mitch said. "You should quit. This thing's going to be very real."

"I'll quit as soon as 'this thing' pays real money," Jason said. "Last time I checked, YouTube was free."

"Yeah, but it's going to lead to everything. Get over here and let's plot some things."

"Thirty seconds!" Mona called, tapping her watch.

"Are you free tomorrow night?" Mitch asked.

"Yeah, unless Mona gets mad and adds me to the schedule. I should go."

"Here's what I'm thinking," Mitch continued. "My mom's working at the hospital tomorrow night. Saturday night, you know? So we play at my house, invite some people over so they can dance, like a party. As long as we straighten the place up before she gets home at six A.M., she'll never know."

"Okay, I'll call you back--" Jason began.

"So we need a bunch of people here," Mitch said.

"I know some people to call." Jason thought of the phone numbers stuffed in his pocket. "I might have more by the end of the night."

"Make sure there's plenty of girls," Mitch said. "We want it to look pretty, you know? And we need somebody with a good camera."

Mona tapped her foot loudly on the pavement. Jason hurried her way.

"I think Tadd Gruber has stuff like that," Jason said. "He's in the A/V club and everything."

"Sounds good. Get him here." Jason stepped toward the door, but Mona blocked him with her fist.

"*No cell phones!*" Mona shrieked.

"Sorry!" Jason hung up, and she moved a step to let him inside.

Jason returned Tadd's laptop to him. "Hey, Tadd, you have a video camera, right?"

"Oh, yeah. Canon VIXIA Camcorder, full HD, a ten-x lens--"

"Is it good for recording sound?"

"I can get some microphones from the A/V room at school. There's a sweet Soundcraft LX7ii mixing board, too--"

"Can you get them by tomorrow night?" Jason asked.

"Sure. The school janitor owes me a favor."

Jason didn't even want to ask about that. "Great. Want to direct our new video?"

"I'm your guy." Tadd winked and made a gun with his fingers. "I'm ready to shoot ya."

"Right. Thanks." Jason walked toward the front counter.

"Hey, Jason?" Tadd called. "Erin's gonna be there, right?"

"We're all going to be there."

"Can't wait to frame her up in my lens. Bam! Hot stuff!" Tadd made a squarish frame shape with his hands and looked at Jason through it.

Jason was already starting to regret asking Tadd.

"Welcome to Buddy McSlawburger's," Jason said as he stepped up to the counter. "Would you like to try the Slawburger Special?"

Chapter Fifteen

After he got home from work, Jason lay back on his bed and took the thick wad of napkins and McSlawburger's receipts from his pocket. Nine girls from his school had given him their phone numbers, none of whom had ever spoken to him before. He had a ready crowd for the video.

Jason turned out his light and closed his eyes. He needed sleep, but he was too excited. He would see Erin tomorrow, and he could only imagine how happy the unexpected jolt of internet fame was making her. All because of the instruments Jason had snagged from the fairies. He imagined her hugging him, maybe getting really happy and kissing him...even if that didn't happen, it was going to be a fun Saturday night, with everybody coming to hear them play.

He lay in the dark for a couple hours, and then he heard a scratching sound, like some kind of animal was crawling under his bed. Jason flipped on his lamp, leaned over the side of his bed, and raised the cover to look underneath.

There was nothing but dust and dirty clothes. Unfortunately, this meant his guitar was missing.

Jason sat up quickly. Just past the foot of his bed, he could see his guitar case floating towards his bedroom window.

"Hey!" Jason hopped off the bed. A pair of small green hands held the guitar case from underneath. Legs dressed in patched, dirty wool trousers ran the guitar closer to the window.

"Stop!" Jason yelled. Remembering how far the goblin could teleport, Jason jumped right in front of the window, instead of directly at the little man.

It worked. The goblin disappeared in a puff, then reappeared on the windowsill, swaying under the weight of the guitar case. Jason snatched the guitar case away. Grizlemor looked up at him in surprise, still stooped over and holding up his empty hands.

"What are you doing?" Jason asked.

"Er, ah..." Grizlemor said.

"Why are you stealing my guitar?"

"Oh, *your* guitar?" Grizlemor chuckled, but it sounded fake. He looked scared. "That's funny. I'm only stealing back what you stole!"

"I just need it a little while longer," Jason said. "We're going to make a video."

"Oh, you are not!" Grizlemor's eyes widened. "Are you trying to pull the wrath of Mad Queen Mab down on your head?"

"Who?"

"The queen of the Fairies! I already explained this."

"Why would she care?" Jason asked.

"Why would she...why would she *care*?" The goblin paced back on forth on Jason's windowsill, shaking his head. "You don't know what you've gotten into, do you? The fairies are right. Man-world has forgotten all about the Folk."

"The who?"

"All of us!" Grizlemor thumped his chest. "Goblins, fairies, elves, dwarves, leprechauns, gnomes...perhaps trolls, if you want to be generous..."

"Oh, little magic people."

"In any case, young sir, kindly hand back that guitar, which is stolen fairy property, and I will restore it to the proper owners."

"Yeah, right," Jason said. "You'll probably just sell it."

"I will not! You have my word."

"But you're a thief," Jason said. "And a...goblin. I can't trust you."

"You, too, are a thief," Grizlemor said. "And a human, the least trustworthy thing of all."

"I'm not giving the guitar back." Jason carried it back toward his bed.

Grizlemor appeared on Jason's bed in a puff of green smoke, pulling at his dirty knots of hair. "But think of the damage raw, unleashed elemental magic could do to this world! In the hands of untrained amateurs!"

"What kind of magic?" Jason asked.

"He doesn't even know!" Grizlemor flopped back on Jason's bed, covering his arm with his eyes and kicking his feet. "How could this happen? Why me, Fates?"

"Why do you even care?" Jason asked. "You're a thief, so you can't really be mad that I stole something. And it's not like I stole from you. Why don't you relax?"

"Relax!" Grizlemor shouted, pounding Jason's bed with both fists.

"Quiet!" Jason whispered. "You'll wake everybody up."

Grizlemor rolled over to lay on his side, looking at Jason. "There are Queensguard all over the city," the goblin said. "Knocking on every door. 'Have you seen these instruments?' 'Any idea who might have these instruments?' They're looking for the ones you stole, Jason. That means the Queen knows about it."

"But you don't have the instruments," Jason said. "So you don't need to worry."

"I know when I need to worry! How many people do you suppose spotted me leading you, a human brat, through Sidhe City? Not a captive dancer in a fairy ring, mind you, but just a boy, wandering free as you please in the streets? And of course, the Queen must know they were taken out of Faerie."

"How would she know that?" Jason said.

"Because she wouldn't care about simple theft otherwise!" Grizlemor was hopping up and down on the bed now. "If they remained in Faerie, it would be of no concern to her. But if four instruments of high elemental magic are taken off to man-world, then whew, the trouble that would cause! Why did you have to be so greedy? Why couldn't you just wait for your little darling's necklace?"

"I still want that back."

"Oh, oh, I don't think so," Grizlemor said, wagging a finger. "Unless you bring me all four of the instruments, so we can put this whole thing to rest."

"It's not your necklace," Jason said.

"Neither are those instruments yours." Grizlemor kept bouncing on the bed. "This is quite fun, isn't it?"

"Stop it!" Jason grabbed him and pulled him down to a sitting position. "You're making too much noise. Look, I'll give the instruments back when we're done with them."

"And when will that be?"

"I'm not sure."

"I'm sure you're not," Grizlemor said. "Because the music of those instruments is addictive to humans. You won't be able to stop playing them."

"I'm giving them back!" Jason snapped.

"Don't go and make this 'video' of yours," Grizlemor said. "Honestly, please. You'll be endangering yourself and your friends. Including that man-girl you're so sweet on."

"What are you talking about?"

"The one with the emerald necklace. I saw her sleeping. She was hideously ugly, by goblin standards, but I suppose if you're just a human—"

"Shut up!"

"I'm only trying to make things easy for you," Grizlemor said.

"What happens if I don't give them back?" Jason asked.

"Oh, don't consider that. The Queen will unleash terrible monsters to pursue you. The longer you make her wait, the worse it will be. She may even feed you to the beasts of the labyrinth."

"The what?"

"You don't understand the power of those instruments," Grizlemor said. "You know they make people dance and feel happy. There's much more inside them. They contain the powers of the four elements."

"Which four elements?"

"There are only four."

"I'm pretty sure there are more than a hundred," Jason said, thinking of the periodic table in his chemistry class.

"You only need four for magical purposes," Grizlemor said, then waved a hand. "Anyway, it's obviously way beyond your brain-grasp. The point is, you're endangering me, and you're endangering yourself, and your man-girl--"

"Stop calling her that."

"--and the wrath of fairies is not something you want to find yourself crushed underneath," Grizlemor said.

Jason's bedroom door opened.

"Jason?" Katie asked. "Who you talking to?" Then she gaped.

Jason looked from Katie back to his bed. A puff of green smoke remained where Grizlemor had been.

"It was the monster!" Katie said. "I'm telling Mom and Dad!" She turned to run down the hall.

"No, Katie, wait!" Jason chased after her and picked her up. "Shhh! Okay? Shhhh!"

Katie looked at him for a few seconds, then nodded her head.

Jason carried her back to his room, closed the door, and set her down.

"Stay very quiet," Jason whispered.

"Okay," she whispered back.

Jason knelt by his bed and lifted the cover. "Come on out, Grizlemor."

After a moment, Grizlemor crawled out and stood up. Katie gaped at the green-skinned goblin, in his filthy woolen cap and coat.

"Katie, this is Grizlemor," Jason said.

Grizlemor doffed his cap and bowed. "Young lady," he said, and Katie giggled.

"Is he a scary fairy?" Katie asked.

"No, he's a goblin."

"But he's a good goblin."

Grizlemor shrugged. "I'm good at *being* a goblin," he said.

"He's not going to hurt us," Jason said. "But you can't trust him. He's a thief."

Grizlemor looked at Jason and snorted. Jason felt a little guilty, but he hoped Grizlemor wouldn't tell Katie that Jason had stolen the instruments from the fairies.

"Just don't tell Mom and Dad," Jason said. "It'll be okay. He was just leaving." Jason gripped the handle of his guitar case tight. "Right, Grizlemor?"

Grizlemor sighed. "If that's how it must be. But remember my warning. You'll wish you had listened to me, Jason. Good evening, young lady." Grizlemor replaced his cap. He jogged to the window, puffed his way up to the sill, and then vanished in a last puff of green of smoke.

"Oooh," Katie said.

"Yeah, ooh," Jason said. "Try chasing him after he stole something of yours."

"What was his warning?" Katie asked.

"It's nothing."

"It sounded big."

"He just, um...doesn't want me telling anybody I saw him.

Goblins like to keep themselves secret."

"It wasn't about those fairy instruments, was it?" Katie asked. "Do the fairies want them back?"

"No, it's no big deal, Katie. Don't even worry about it."

"Are you in trouble with the fairies?"

"Nobody's in trouble. Just promise me you won't go wake up Mom and Dad. Okay?"

"He's gone, right?"

"He's all gone."

"Will you tuck me in?"

"Fine, whatever." Jason picked her up and carried her to her room. "There. Good night, Katie."

"And read me a story," Katie whispered.

"Katie, I have to go."

"Just a short one."

Jason shook his head, annoyed. He looked at the bright picture books on Katie's bookshelf. "What kind of story do you want?"

"One about fairies," Katie whispered, with a sneaky grin.

Chapter Sixteen

Saturday, Jason woke up worrying over the goblin's warning. It had been hard to take Grizlemor seriously when Jason had just caught him burglarizing his house again. He'd brushed off Grizlemor's warnings as the goblin's attempt to act like he was doing Jason a favor by robbing him.

Now Jason wondered if there might be some truth in what the goblin said. He looked from his guitar case to the heap of napkins with phone numbers on his table. There had to be some kind of price to pay for this, Jason thought. Magic instruments that could draw such a crowd, and turn many more people into fans after hearing just one song—and only half of the song, really, presented in a shaky, poor quality video made on a phone—magic like that couldn't be just free for the taking.

Jason didn't know if he believed Grizlemor's talk about the Fairy Queen, but the fairy musicians themselves would certainly want such amazing instruments back, and could very possibly harbor some fairy fury for the person who stole them.

He remembered the "Queensguard" fairies in their black armor and long swords. Even if they were small, they looked tough and vicious. Jason could probably fight off one or two, but he wouldn't want to get into a fight with a pack of them.

Then his cell phone rang. Mitch.

"All systems go," Mitch said.

"Huh?"

"It's happening tonight," Mitch said. "Tadd's coming over to shoot the video tonight. Call up all those new fans and let them know."

"Are you sure?"

"Yeah, I just got off the phone with Tadd."

"Maybe this isn't a good idea," Jason said. "We don't even know how this magic stuff works."

"But we know it *works*. Don't back out now. Erin's excited about it, too."

Jason rubbed his head. He didn't want to disappoint her.

He opened his case and looked at the enchanted guitar, the strange runes everywhere on the dark, polished wood, the glimmering golden tuning pegs. He brushed his fingertips along the deep engravings on the soundboard, gazing at the sparkling little amethysts that dotted it here and there. The guitar was warm to the touch, like a living thing. It seemed to call to him. He could barely resist the temptation to pick it up and start playing.

His mom knocked on the door. "Jason, the lawn isn't going to mow itself."

"I'll be out in a minute," Jason told her.

"Not yet, my mom's still here," Mitch said on the phone.

"I wasn't talking to you, Mitch."

"*Mick.* Just get us an audience and get yourself here tonight. I'm taking care of everything else." Mitch hung up.

Jason hesitated, then picked up the first napkin and dialed the number.

"Hello?" a girl's voice asked.

"Hi, um…" He checked the name. "Wendy? This is Jason Becker. You gave me your number last night at Buddy McSlawburger's—"

A painfully high-pitched squeal pierced his eardrum, and Jason pulled the phone away from his head. His ear was ringing.

"Are you okay?" Jason asked when he put the phone back to his ear.

"Ooh, yah," she said. "Everything's great. You?"

"I was just letting you know we're playing a show tonight, if you want to come--"

She let out another excited squeal, and Jason pulled the phone away faster this time.

"Oh, this is awesome!" she was saying. "I can't wait! Where?"
Jason gave her Mitch's address.

"This is so perfect! I can't wait to tell everybody on Facebook!"

"It's not going to be huge or anything--"

"It'll be *so* huge!" she shouted. "Eeeeeeeeeeeeeeeeeee!"

"Okay," Jason said. "So, you're coming?"

"I have to go tell everyone!"

"You don't have to tell everyone--" Jason said, but she'd already hung up.

He got a similar response from the second number, and the third.

Late in the afternoon, Jason stuffed his McSlawburger's uniform into his backpack, and told his dad he was going to work. His dad was sitting in his recliner in the living room.

"I thought you were off tonight," his dad said, looking away from the Golf Channel.

"Yeah, they changed my schedule."

"A little bit of short notice, isn't it?"

"Mona hates me. That's the assistant manager. I guess somebody must have called in sick, or quit." Jason shrugged.

"You know you're still grounded," his dad said. "You'd better not be sneaking off with your friends."

"I'm not."

"Stay out of trouble." His dad turned his attention back to the golf game.

Jason stopped by the garage, where he'd stashed his guitar so his parents wouldn't see him leaving with it, then rode his bike across town to Buddy McSlawburger's. He changed into his uniform and stood at the drive-through, letting a sophomore named Lizzy Mueller take a long break. Jason wasn't scheduled tonight, but Lizzy had been more than happy to let Jason work part of her shift for her.

Jason took and filled the drive-through orders until a familiar voice came over the headset: "One cheeseburger, hold the slaw, one Slawchicken Combo, hold the slaw, and an extra-large fry, hold the chili-cheese. One Kiddo McSlawburger Meal...hold the slaw."

"Pull around to the window," Jason said with a grin.

His dad pulled up, and looked both surprised and pleased to see Jason actually at work.

"Hiya, Dad," Jason said. "I thought you hated the burgers here."

"Only when they glop all that disgusting slaw on them," his dad replied. "How's work tonight?"

"Pretty busy." Jason handed over the greasy paper bag of food. "Don't forget to stop for heartburn medicine."

His dad laughed. "How late are you working?"

"Till closing."

A car horn beeped somewhere in the drive-through line.

"Okay, Jayce. Have a good night."

Jason waved as his dad pulled away.

As soon as there was a break in the drive-through customers, Jason found Lizzy reading a bright tabloid at one table in the dining room. *CLAUDIA LAFAYETTE: Who is She REALLY Dating Now?* asked the headline.

"Your turn," he said.

"Aw, you sure you don't want to work all night?" Lizzy asked.

"I'd love to, but I'm busy." Jason took off his tall, floppy hat and rubbed his sweaty scalp underneath. "Thanks, Lizzy!"

"You can work for me anytime, eh?" Lizzy said with a smile. She walked behind the counter, and Jason went to the bathroom. He changed back into his jeans and black T-shirt, shoved his uniform in his backpack, then went outside and unchained his bike from the rack.

He hurried to Mitch's neighborhood.

Chapter Seventeen

Jason was running late, but not by much. He was glad his dad had actually come to check on him, or he would have been stuck at the drive-through until nine or ten, when his parents usually went to bed.

Mitch's mom's car was gone from the driveway. The garage door was closed, but the front door stood wide open. Jason opened the glass storm door and walked inside.

"Doorbell!" Jason announced as he stepped into the house. "Where are you, Mitch?"

"It's *Mick*. Back here in the living room."

Jason was surprised to walk into the small living room and find Mitch's silvery keyboards and computer set up near the stairs to the second floor. Portions of Dred's drum kit had been moved inside, too. Mitch was wiring in amplifiers while Tadd taped microphones to the walls.

"Jayce!" Tadd said, a nickname that annoyed Jason. "Welcome to the soundstage, baby!"

"Hi, Tadd." Jason looked at Mitch. "Is Erin here?"

"She'll be here, man," Mitch said. "It's Dred we have to worry about."

"Dred?"

"Yeah, you call her," Mitch said. "She says she doesn't want to come. I'm moving her drums in here, anyway."

"Why are we in the living room?"

"Better atmosphere," Tadd said. "Ambient lighting, more windows...it looks like a real house."

"It is a real house," Jason said.

"I think it's going to really symbolize breaking out of the boring routine of suburban life and really going wild," Tadd said. "It's a perfect environment for that visual message. I mean, look at the tchotchke shelf. The perfect representation of the dull and mundane."

"When did you become Steven Spielberg?" Jason asked.

"Spielberg?" Tadd snorted. "The true art of film died with Federico Fellini."

"Are you calling Dred or not?" Mitch asked Jason.

"Why doesn't she want to come?" Jason took out his phone.

"She'll have to explain it to you. I sure don't understand."

Jason dialed Dred's number.

"Yeah," Dred answered.

"How's it going?" Jason asked.

"Did Mitch put you up to calling me?" she asked.

"Oh, no. I'm just wondering when you're coming. Everyone's supposed to be here by nine, so we should be ready to play by then."

"I'm not coming," Dred said.

"You're not?"

"Like Mitch didn't already tell you."

"Why wouldn't you come?" Jason asked. "That crummy video Mitch's neighbor shot is already super-popular. There's a bunch of people who want to hear more of our music. This is our chance."

"It's not our music," Dred said.

"What do you mean?"

"You were too busy playing to notice," Dred said. "It didn't sound like our normal music at all. They aren't coming to hear us, Jason. They're coming to hear those creepy instruments."

"Who cares? They want to see our band."

"I care. There's something supernatural about those things."

"Yeah, I told you, I got them from fairies," Jason said. "And everybody loves them."

"Don't you know any stories about fairies?" Dred asked.

"Um...Peter Pan?"

"I mean real stories," Dred said. "I've been reading about them all night. You can't trust them. They're dangerous and tricky, according to all the old stories. If that's where the instruments came from—and after Thursday, I kind of believe you—then we could be in a lot of danger."

Her words reminded him of Grizlemor's warning. Jason shook his head to clear the thought.

"It's just one show, Dred," Jason said. "Just a small party. You can come for one night. Just play your regular drums, if you don't want to use the one I gave you. But we really need you."

"I'm busy."

"With what?"

"I'm *packing*. I'm moving to St. Paul in a few days. Already have a roommate and everything."

"Really?"

"Did you think I was kidding about moving away?" Dred asked.

"Then just play this one show with us," Jason said. "Please? I've got so many people coming. It's going to be humiliating if the band's not here. Please, Dred? As a favor?"

Dred was quiet for a minute, then she sighed.

"Just this one time," Dred said. "And I'm playing my own drums, not that haunted one."

"Great! Thanks!"

"Don't let Mitch touch my drum kit."

"Right..." Jason watched Mitch carry one of Dred's toms into the room and set it into place. "So when will you get here?"

"Give me half an hour. I can't believe I'm doing this." Dred hung up.

The doorbell rang, and Mitch told Jason to get it.

Three girls at the front door shrieked when they saw him. Jason recognized one as Wendy, the first girl who'd given Jason her number the previous night.

"Hi," Jason said, opening the storm door. "The party doesn't start for like an hour..."

"Then why are all these people here?" Wendy asked.

"What people?"

Wendy pointed, and Jason leaned out to look. Cars were parking all along Mitch's street, with excited kids climbing out of them. A gang of ten or twelve freshman were walking up the street, arriving on foot. It might have been thirty people in all.

"Oh, wow," Jason said. "Come on in."

He led the three girls into the living room, and they shrieked again when they saw Mitch.

"We have guests coming," Jason said. "A ton of people are here already."

"How many did you invite?" Mitch asked.

"Maybe ten. But I told them to bring friends. And it looks like they all brought three or four."

"What?" Mitch stood up behind his keyboard. "That's too many. We only need fifteen or twenty."

"Hi!" Wendy and her friends approached Mitch. "You're Mitch, right?"

"*Mick.*"

"Mick!" the three girls exclaimed.

"Can we get a pic with you?" Wendy asked.

"I guess." Mitch looked confused.

The girls gathered in around him, putting their arms around them, then took pictures with their phones, acting excited, as if they'd met an actual rock star.

People started flooding in through the front door. They swarmed Mitch and Jason, demanding to hear music.

"Wait, wait," Mitch said. "Everybody, we're still getting set up here."

The crowd grumbled.

"We came to hear the band!" one guy shouted.

"Just wait!" Mitch said.

"Come on, play!" a girl yelled, and the crowd voiced their agreement with her.

"Half the band isn't even here yet!" Mitch said. He was looking agitated at the swelling crowd that filled his house.

"Play something!" another guy yelled.

"Jason," Mitch said, "Can you give them a guitar solo or something?"

"Do it!" Wendy yelled. She was grasping Mitch's hand tight, while Mitch tried to pull away.

"Okay, whatever." Jason opened his guitar case, and he jumped when a number of people cheered and clapped. It seemed ridiculous that they could be reacting so strongly to a band nobody had heard of even two days earlier. Especially when the band was just a group of kids from their own town. It was unreal, and a little scary.

Jason sat down on the couch, and girls pushed their way in all around him, sitting beside him, behind him on the couch back, and all around his feet. They stared at him expectantly.

"So, here's something I like to warm up with," Jason said.

"Yeah, warm up!" one girl shouted.

"Warm up!" another added.

"Hurry!"

"You have to give me a little space," Jason said, but nobody backed up. He drew his pick across all six strings, filling the air with sound, and the whole crowd seemed to sigh and relax.

He played "Learning to Fly" by Tom Petty, one of the first songs he'd learned on guitar. The people around him cheered at a volume that made Jason's ears ring.

"Sing!" a girl yelled from the back of the crowd.

"I don't really sing," Jason said. "Our singer's on the way here."

"Sing anyway!" a guy shouted.

"Um, I'll try..." Jason sang the first line haltingly, but then the words starting pouring out of his mouth with no effort. The guitar vibrations seemed to strengthen his singing voice, making it sound almost decent. The crowd joined in and sang along with him, and the girls around him leaned in closer, as if they went to going to gang up and smother him. Tadd was circling around, getting footage of Jason and the crowd.

The guitar grew warm in his hands, and the air grew thick and hot, like there wasn't enough oxygen for all the people packed into the room. Still, he kept singing with no trouble.

Then Erin walked into the room. Unfortunately, she was with her boyfriend Zach.

Jason stopped playing and stood up, struggling to find some fresh air to breathe.

"There's our singer!" Jason said. "So she'll be singing from now on. This is the end of the part where I sing."

The crowd turned and gasped, then closed in around Erin. The guys seemed particularly interested in getting close to her.

"Sing!" somebody yelled.

"Yeah, sing a song for us!"

"You're so pretty!"

"You really are!"

"I love you!"

Zach gaped at all the dopey-eyed fanboys congregated around his girlfriend. Jason took more than a little pleasure in his discomfort.

Erin approached Mitch. Zach followed, trying to elbow guys out of his way while maintaining his photo-perfect smile.

"This is a huge crowd!" Erin said to Mitch, speaking loudly over the chattering, excited mob. "Where did they all come from?"

Mitch pointed to Jason. "He invited them."

"Very impressive, Jason!" Erin called, while Jason tried to ease his way past adoring fans to reach the other band members.

"I only called a few people."

"What about all the people outside?" Erin asked. "Where are they going to listen?"

"There's *more* outside?" Mitch looked horrified.

"Like a hundred people," Erin said.

"My mom's going to kill me." Mitch looked like he wanted to bang his head against something.

"We should open the windows and turn on the ceiling fans," Jason said. "It's going to get really hot in here."

The crowd cheered at his words, which he hardly expected. Guests hurried to open up the windows, as if Jason had given an order and they were obedient servants. The breeze from outside cooled things down a little. People were already crowded outside the windows, and they applauded when then windows opened.

"This is crazy," Erin said.

"Did all these people really come to see you?" Zach said. "Maybe we should get out of here. This is weird."

"Hey, hands off!" Dred shouted. She'd entered the room, and she used both her drumsticks to beat back the reaching hands of admiring fans. "Where did all these people come from, Mitch?"

"*Mick.* This is our fan base! Like 'em?"

"I don't know." Dred whacked a hand from her sleeve with the end of a drumstick. She pushed forward until she was standing in front of her drum kit. "Who moved my drums?"

"We were running out of time."

"And who's this guy?" She jabbed a drumstick at Tadd, who was following her with the camera. He barely dodged it.

"Tadd's shooting the video," Jason said.

"I know you said you didn't want this, but I brought it out just in case." Mitch handed the little fairy drum to Dred, who scowled at it for a second, then put it aside on the tchotchke shelf, among porcelain cats and glass angels.

"Don't need it," Dred said. Then she crossed her arms and

stared at a freshman girl who sat on the stool behind the drum kit, gazing in admiration at Mitch. "Hey, shove off, creampuff!"

The girl jumped, looked at Dred and the sticks in her hands, and scurried off, though she couldn't go far in the dense crowd.

"Hey, everybody?" Mitch said, waving his arms. "If you could just back up a step or two, we can get warmed up here."

"Come on, make room for the band!" Tadd said, waving his camera. "And me! Lots of room for me!"

"Hey, what's the band called, anyway?" a girl asked Mitch.

"Yeah, what's it called? What's it called?" more girls asked, grabbing at Mitch's hand and arm.

"We're the Assorted Zebras," Mitch said.

"That's a great name!"

"Awesome name!"

"The Assorted Zebras! I love it so much!" the first girl said, leaning close to Mitch and gazing at his chin.

"Well, we call it that because the zebra can't be tamed," Mitch said. "You can't ride a zebra, or make it pull a plow, or anything. The zebra is the Mick Jagger of the equine world. If you look into the history of sub-Saharan Africa, you'll find that the wildness of the zebra as compared to the horse was actually a major economic setback for thousands of years--"

"Just play already!" a guy shouted.

The crowd closed in tighter around the band.

Mitch played a few notes on the keyboard, and the crowd quieted a bit. Jason strummed his guitar, and Erin took out her harmonica and warmed it up. Jason didn't need to touch his golden tuning pegs—the instruments tuned to each other automatically, and an electric resonance crackled through the room.

"Okay, everybody, thanks for coming out!" Erin shouted. "We are the Assorted Zebras."

The crowd applauded.

"I guess we'll start with 'Cinderella Night,'" Erin said. "That's the one from the video you all saw."

The crowd cheered like it was an old favorite.

Dred tapped out a four-count, and then the rest of the band jumped in. As before, the sound was powerful with the three magic instruments working together. Jason felt alternating chills and blasts of heat rushing up his spine. His hands became very loose and relaxed, and the guitar strings almost seemed to bend up to meet his fingertips and his pick, as if the guitar were eager to make music.

The crowd thrashed to the song, screaming along with Erin's lyrics. It sounded like they'd all memorized the words.

The music worked its magic on Jason, too, so that soon he thought of nothing, but lost himself in the playing.

At the end of the song, the crowd applauded and cheered and stomped. The people gathered at the windows pounded their hands against the screens and window frames.

"Go easy on my house!" Mitch shouted. Then he pointed at a group of senior guys across the room, who were opening brown bottles. "Hey, no beer! I'm serious!"

The guys toasted Mitch as though he'd greeted them.

"Okay, here's a song I wrote for my boyfriend Zach here." Erin touched Zach's shoulder, and he gave the crowd an annoyed half-smile.

Erin sang, and the crowd went wild. They were dancing everywhere: on the coffee table, the stairs, up against the walls, knocking down the framed pictures. Mitch shook his head, but he kept playing. He slowly closed his eyes, and it looked like he was getting lost in the music like Jason.

Jason smiled and closed his eyes, too, letting the song direct his hands and fingers. Playing the guitar was effortless. He somehow never missed a beat, never got a chord wrong, but it felt like all he was doing was listening and letting the music flow through him.

Erin moved on to "Remember," which had everybody crying and holding each other by the final verse.

"Okay, sorry, let's pick things up a little," Erin said, wiping tears from her face. She played the opening for "Roller Coaster" on her harmonica. It was a much faster song and at least sounded upbeat, unless you listened too closely to the lyrics about being thrown around by your emotions.

Jason and Mitch played along, but there was no drumbeat. Jason looked back at Dred, and she was swaying as if hypnotized by the music, her eyes closing.

"Dred!" he said in a loud stage whisper. "Dred, wake up!"

"Huh?" Dred's eyes fluttered open, but they had a blank, empty look. She gazed around the room, then saw the drumsticks in her hand. "Oh! Sorry." She started tapping the rhythm.

A pair of uniformed police officers elbowed their way into the crowd. One of them pointed to the kids drinking beer, and both the cops started in that direction. Jason looked at Mitch, then Erin, but they were both deep into the music, their eyes closed.

The drumbeat stopped—then resumed, but stronger and deeper than before. Jason looked back.

Dred had placed the little fairy drum in her lap and started hitting it with her fingertips. It grew larger as she played, and the sound became more thunderous.

It swelled into a full-size snare drum, inscribed everywhere with fairy runes, with some kind of animal hide stretched taut across the top.

Jason looked back at the two cops, but they'd both joined in the dancing, their eyes closed, drawn into the music like everyone else. Jason smiled.

Dred stopped playing long enough to lift the original snare drum from her kit and toss it aside like a piece of garbage. She replaced it with the fairy drum. She resumed playing, and the drum kit slowly changed. As with Mitch's keyboard set-up, the fairy instrument seemed to infect the other instruments. The two toms slowly shifted form until they resembled the fairy drum, wooden with runes. The cymbal and hi-hat turned to gold. Finally, the big bass drum shifted its appearance, too.

On the front of the bass drum, a hieroglyphic image of zebras appeared. The zebras were animated, and they ran faster as Dred accelerated the tempo. Words appeared above the moving images like twisting smoke: THE ASSORTED ZEBRAS.

The crowd cheered at the special effects. Jason felt his guitar grow hot. With all four instruments playing together, a kind of magical haze seemed to fall over the room, charging the air with energy. The dancing audience synced up with each other so that they appeared almost choreographed.

Jason felt the crowd's growing energy course through him like fire.

Erin lowered her harmonica and sang new lyrics he'd never heard before. His fingers played a tune that matched it perfectly.

Let tonight last forever
Capture my sound and song
Share it with your world
Pass the song along...

As if Erin's words were a spell, everybody took out their phones and began recording the show.

There is no pain
We'll always stay young
Forget your past
And the days to come...

Erin's new song was like a lullaby for the mind. The words and music filled Jason with a deep, warm bliss, blanking out his mind.

Erin reached the end of her verses and starting playing harmonica again. Dred's drumming grew faster and faster—bass, toms, cymbals, snare, all somehow ringing out at once. Her eyes seemed to glow with a kind of mania as her hands and drumsticks flew everywhere. Sweat soaked the kerchief tied to her head and drenched all of her clothes.

Jason, Erin, and Mitch gave up trying to follow her. They surrendered, letting Dred tear off into a wild, loud, crashing drum solo.

The floor rumbled under their feet. Each time Dred hit the cymbal, a window shattered, or a porcelain cat exploded with a sound like a gunshot.

The house shook as Dred's tempo accelerated to an inhuman speed. Deep cracks spread up the walls. Puffs of plaster rained down from the ceiling—but she didn't stop playing, nobody stopped dancing, and the rest of the band was just as enthralled as the audience.

The house shuddered like it was caught in an earthquake. The stairway railing splintered and broke into pieces. Light fixtures and lamps blew out, and the ceiling fan swung wildly. The plaster ceiling cracked and fell in big chunks.

As Dred hit her crescendo, the entire house bucked and heaved, seeming to lift up from the ground—and then with a final crashing sound, the interior walls came tumbling down, exposing the wooden frame of the house and all the pipes and wiring.

Dred threw her sticks at her snare drum, where they bounced off and whirled away through the air.

There was a long beat of silence.

Then the entire crowd erupted, cheering and screaming their heads off, clapping and stomping and banging their fists on everything in sight. It was deafening.

It lasted several minutes. When the crowd finally died down, Erin said, "Thanks for coming everyone! We're the Assorted Zebras. Good night!"

Mitch and Dred stood up and joined Jason and Erin in a bow, and the applause reignited.

"Did you get all that?" Mitch asked Tadd.

"Oh, yeah," Tadd said quietly, shaking his head. "We got it all."

"Come on, let's mix the video on my desktop. I want this uploaded tonight!" Mitch led the way upstairs, past confused-looking kids who crowded the steps.

Dred sat down, leaned against the wall, and closed her eyes in exhaustion.

Jason and Erin looked at each while little bits of the house continued to drop around them.

"Uh...do you think Mitch noticed what happened to his house?" Erin asked.

"I'm pretty sure he'll pick up on it eventually," Jason said.

"That was completely wild!" Zach grabbed Erin and gave her a long kiss. "I didn't know you could really sing."

"I told you," Erin said. "You don't listen."

"Let's get out of this place before it falls on our heads," Zach said. "We should all get going, for safety."

Dred groaned.

"Do you need some water, Dred?" Jason asked.

Dred raised a finger without opening her eyes. Jason took it as a "yes."

"It actually might be dangerous here," Erin said, looking at the exposed ribs of the house, the deteriorating ceiling. "Maybe we should go."

The crowd was dispersing. Clumps of quiet, exhausted, confused-looking kids wandered outside, not talking very much. The two cops were among them, their eyes drooping as if they would keel over asleep any second. Jason remembered the kids who'd been brought down to Faerie for the night so the fairies could drain their energy with music.

"Wait a second." Jason hurried into the kitchen, which looked like it had been struck by a tornado. The cabinets sagged forward from the walls with their doors hanging open. The dishes inside had crashed all over the counter and floor. Two large cracks, each more than an inch wide, ran all the way across the floor, breaking it into three uneven levels.

Jason stepped carefully to the counter. He found a plastic cup, shook fragments of coffee mug out of it, and filled it with cool water.

By the time he returned to the living room and handed the water to Dred, Zach and Erin were stepping out the front door. The rest of the guests were leaving, too, with dazed, zombie-like looks on their faces.

"Hey, wait, Erin." Jason ran after her. "Why don't you stay? We can look at Tadd's video."

"I'm really just worried about this house collapsing," Erin pointed to the sagging, broken ceiling overhead. "We should go

"We have to meet Gustav and Muppet Boy at the coffee shop, like, thirty minutes ago," Zach said.

"Just stay here," Jason said.

"Um..." Erin looked at the broken ceiling and walls again, then at her boyfriend.

"Let's go." Zach jingled his keychain as he walked out the door.

Erin backed out the door, still looking at Jason. "You'll let me know when it's done, right? Send the link to my phone?"

"Yep," Jason said.

"Thanks." Erin looked past him and waved. "Bye, Dred!"

Dred, still sitting against the wall, raised her empty cup and shook it. Jason walked over to get her a refill, but he kept his eyes on Erin.

"Bye, Jason." She gave him a tired smile. Her blonde and green and blue hair was dark with sweat, plastered against her head. "That was a great show, wasn't it?"

"A great show," Jason agreed, and he tried to smile as he watched her leave.

Jason watched the last stragglers stumble their way across Mitch's front lawn and off into the night. The cars drove past, each one bouncing as it hit a huge chasm that spread across the front yard and out into the street. It ended in a spiderweb crack of asphalt in the center of the street. Jason shook his head at the destruction.

Up and down the streets, neighbors had come out onto the porches and driveway, gaping at Mitch's house.

Jason ran inside and went upstairs, careful to avoid the splintered handrail, and walked into Mitch's room.

Mitch and Tadd were hunkered over Mitch's desktop,

whispering excitedly to each other as they cut and rearranged the video file. Snips and snarls of music thumped over the speakers as they mixed the sound from the different microphones.

Two Claudia Lafayette posters hung over the bed. One showed her with sea-green eyes and a matching dress, soaking wet on a rock in the ocean, the green dress clinging to her legs to suggest a mermaid's tale. In another poster, she had violet eyes and a leather jacket, and leaned against a black motorcycle with an ornate violet painted on the engine.

"She must have a closet full of contact lenses," Jason joked, pointing at the posters. Neither Mitch nor Tadd acknowledged he'd spoken.

The doorbell rang.

"What's that?" Mitch said.

"Oh, yeah," Jason told him. "All your neighbors are probably coming over to see what happened."

Mitch opened the door, walked down the now-crooked hallway to the top of the steps, and screamed.

Jason and Tadd ran out after him.

"What's wrong?" Jason asked.

"Look at my house!" Mitch shouted. He pointed at the uneven steps, the shattered handrail, the broken floor and furniture and walls. "What happened?"

The doorbell rang again.

"You were here," Jason said. "It was the music."

"Yeah, man," Tadd said. "We just watched that happen again on the video."

"Yeah, but this is real." Mitch closed his eyes and rubbed his forehead with his hands. "Wow."

"You didn't notice before?" Jason asked.

"I don't know," Mitch said. "It just didn't seem like it was actually happening."

The ceiling fan pulled loose from it housing and crashed into the coffee table.

"Oh, I wish I'd been shooting that," Tadd said.

"My mom is going to kill me," Mitch said. "Then she's going to hire a necromancer to raise me from the dead so she can kill me again."

"Just tell her it was a freak earthquake," Tadd said.

The doorbell rang several times, insistently.

"Great. Now I just need a whole construction crew to rebuild the house in the next couple of hours." Mitch shook his head. "You guys better get out of here."

"I'll help clean up," Jason said.

"I don't think 'cleaning up' is really going to touch the problem here," Mitch said. "Just go. I don't want the neighbors telling my mom I had people over. She'll go mental."

"She's not supposed to be home for a couple of hours, though, right?" Jason asked.

"Sure. If the neighbors haven't called her yet. How did I not realize this was happening?"

"The music," Jason said. "It plays with your mind."

"Seriously, go on," Mitch said. The doorbell rang yet again. "Try not to let my neighbors see you leave."

"You sure?" Jason asked.

"Yes! Go!"

"All right, man, we's out." Tadd held up a hand for a high-five, but Mitch was not in a high-fiving mood.

Jason packed up his guitar and walked out the back door with Tadd. They circled around to the front of the house. Jason had to get his bike from the garage, and he saw several of Mitch's neighbors on the front porch. An old man in a bathrobe was punching the doorbell again and again.

"When did Dred leave?" Jason whispered. Her van was gone.

"Probably when everyone else did." Tadd pointed towards his car, a rusty sedan. "Want a ride?"

"Thanks," Jason said. Tadd opened the trunk, and Jason loaded the bike inside. They drove past several outraged-looking neighbors, who approached the car and tried to wave them down, but Tadd ignored them and drove on.

He could barely keep his eyes open on the drive home.

Chapter Eighteen

It was dark over the town of Glastonbury, the deep, brooding clouds smothering the light of the moon and stars. From the top of the lone hill, the dark plains of Somerset stretched away into the night. The only sound was a drum circle of hippies near the base of the hill.

A roofless rock tower, three stories high, sat atop the hill, with two doorless archways facing each other so wind and people could pass right through. The floor was worn stone, the tiles cracked and aged with time. One of these tiles had risen up and tilted back like the lid of a trap door, revealing a squarish hole in the floor.

The elf named Hokealussiplatytorpinquarnartnuppy Melaerasmussanatolinkarrutorpicus Darnathiopockettlenocbiliotroporiqqua Bellefrost raised his head out of the floor hole and gazed out at the dark expanse beyond the archway. He looked up at the dark sky above the tower, then back at the archway behind him. So far, there was no sign of a guardian, but appearances could deceive.

He climbed out onto the floor of the roofless tower. The unicorn's pink horn and mane rose from the hole behind him, and she turned her head from one side to the other, taking in the scene with watchful, chocolate-drop eyes.

"Stay there, Buttercake," Hoke whispered. "I'll check for a guard."

Hoke walked out through one archway. A single ribbon of concrete stretched from the ruins of the tower down to the lowlands beneath it. The rest of the hill was blank, covered in grass.

Hoke shook his head as he walked a complete circle around the tower. The place had changed a great deal since the last time he was here. It looked uninhabited, maybe even unguarded, but Hoke kept his hand on his belt anyway. Pouches of combat herbs and a sharp, sheathed flint blade lay within easy reach.

He stepped back into archway where he'd begun.

"Come along, Buttercake," he said. The unicorn emerged cautiously, swishing her pink tail, and eased toward him. "Don't forget to shut the door," Hoke added.

Buttercake snorted. She walked back and kicked the stone tile, and it moved back into place.

"Good girl," Hoke said. He scratched her mane as she joined him in the doorway. She turned her head to nuzzle his hand.

They walked out onto the concrete path and started down the hill at an easy pace.

"I don't suppose you've been to man-world, have you?" Hoke asked.

Buttercake neighed.

"And you're too young to remember the wars," Hoke said. "You wouldn't believe me, but this very place where you're clomping was once a large city of fairies. Maybe the largest."

Buttercake made a blowing sound and shook her head.

"Oh, yes," Hoke said. "Down there, those grassy terraces? Each one was a street more crowded than any thoroughfare in Sidhe City. All manner of Folk were welcome here—fairies, elves, 'chauns and gnomes, all in peace together. It was called *Ynys yr Afalon*. In time, just 'Avalon,' because everyone likes to shorten things. That was in the time of Mad Mab's grandfather, the good fairy king Gwynn ap Nudd. Many thousands of years gone," Hoke sighed. Seeing the place so empty made his heart ache. The world had once been very different, and kinder.

Buttercake stopped and sniffed the grass by the walkway.

"Smell the residual magic everywhere, don't you?" Hoke asked. He looked out over the lowlands again. "The hill used to be an island in the sea. Then a lake. 'Course, the fairies took everything after the Iron Wars, took the other layer of this hill, the whole city, Avalon— that's the Old Town Quarter in Sidhe City, now."

Buttercake gave him a questioning whinny and resumed walking. The path ran along a shallow slope of the hill, so it was a longer route than if they'd walked down one of the steep sides.

"It's hard to explain," Hoke answered. "Humans and Folk lived in peace for as long as anyone remembers. Then the humans began attacking us with iron, taking our land, so we all fled together."

Buttercake gave a sad, soft blow.

"It is unfortunate," Hoke agreed. "But humans are about as trustworthy as fairies. That's why I like the swamp, just me and you cornhorses. Nobody bothers us."

They were halfway down the hill now, slowly approaching the ring of humans beating their drums.

"We'd better get out of sight," Hoke said. He hopped on the unicorn's back, stroking her neck. Thousands of little sparkles gleamed in her pink horn, and then the elf and the unicorn turned invisible together. Buttercake stepped off the path to walk quietly in the grass, so her cloven hooves didn't ring on the concrete.

The humans in the drum circle were a mingling of males and females, a range of ages. They all had quite long hair, many of them twisted into thick braids or dreadlocks. Some of them were singing.

They reminded him, strangely, of the primitive, friendly humans from the Age of Flint, before the horrible Age of Iron. Of course, you couldn't believe anything you saw among the humans. Their world was full of illusions.

One of the drummers stood up and stretched. He had thick gray dreadlocks, a grizzled beard, tired-looking eyes. His airbrushed t-shirt read "*Ask me about* **Glastonbury Tours**!"

Hoke touched the back of Buttercake's neck. She stopped walking and stood still.

The dreadlocked man staggered away from the group of drummers as if drunk. Once he was several paces away from them, however, he stood up straight and walked with purpose. His eyes scanned along the concrete path, up the rocky hill to the tower at the top. Hoke held his breath.

The man's eyes turned solid black. His jaw opened, revealing teeth that were suddenly long and sharp, almost too big for his mouth. Then a forked tongue uncoiled between his teeth and reached out until it was longer than his arms. The tongue swirled in the air, tasting it like a snake.

It had to be the guardian, Hoke thought. And he didn't have the hexagonal gold and black medallion to indicate he was on official business for Queen Mab. He was on unofficial business, so he couldn't reveal a thing to the guardian. The Queen clearly wanted the missing magical instruments kept quiet. That was probably why she'd hired a solitary elf like Hoke, who wouldn't be spreading the story to anyone, except maybe some giant sugarcane trees.

Hoke felt Buttercake tense beneath him, afraid. He rubbed her between the shoulders to try and calm her.

The Queen enforced the Supreme Law, or at least the part forbidding anyone from Faerie from crossing into man-world. To this end, she appointed darkfae to guard the doors between the worlds. These were fairies who'd been twisted into evil, wicked things, usually by too much exposure to black magic. Trolls, boggarts, dullahans...nasty things.

The creature currently approaching him was known as a *boggart*, known for being unstable and very violent. Apparently, it kept itself disguised among the humans in order to keep an eye on the gate.

The boggart spun its long tongue through the air again. Then it sucked the tongue back inside, and its teeth shrunk a little, though they remained much longer and sharper than a human's.

"Who's out there, then?" the boggart asked.

Hoke and Buttercup remained still and quiet.

"The Glastonbury Door is closed," the boggart with gray dreadlocks said. "Queen's Law. No Folk out, no tallboys in." He stalked up the hill, sniffing the air with his tongue again. "Who's being naughty? Goblin? Elf? Smells like elf to me."

Hoke tapped Buttercup's right side. She turned to the right and started down the slope, away from the concrete path where the boggart was walking.

"I am the guardian of the gate, appointed by the Queensguard," the boggart hissed as he climbed. "You go back as you came, or we'll give you the iron." He drew a long dagger from inside his high leather boot.

Hoke gave Buttercake three quick taps, and the unicorn hurried down the slope.

The boggart continued up the path, past the point where Hoke and Buttercake had turned away. It stopped after a few steps and unfurled its tongue to its full length, tasting the air again.

"Oh, aren't we a clever one?" the boggart asked as he backtracked. The tips of his forked tongue brushed the grass near his feet, just where Buttercake had stepped off. The boggart followed, moving directly toward them now. He'd picked up their scent.

Hoke took a pouch from his belt and opened the drawstring. It held sneezewort leaves, dried and crushed into a powder. Unfortunately, it was even drier and older than he expected, and a small puff of dust curled out and floated up to his nostrils.

Hoke sneezed, not just once, but a dozen times in a row, each one echoing like a thunderclap inside his nose. He felt Buttercake tense up beneath him, her muscles swelling. She was about to panic.

When Hoke finally managed to stop sneezing and open his itchy, tear-filled eyes, he saw the blurry shape of the boggart charging at them, teeth extended to full length, iron dagger raised and ready to strike.

Hoke rubbed Buttercake to sooth her, and with his other hand, he readied the pouch of sneezewort.

"Ha! You're more sneezy than sneaky, then!" the boggart crowed as he approached. His tongue lashed the air all around Hoke and Buttercake. "I smell a naughty elf, and...what's this? A griffin? A dragon? Or, perhaps..."

Hoke dashed the sneezewort at the boggart. The dried powder rolled out in a big cloud, coating the entire length of the boggart's tongue.

"What's this?" the boggart managed to say, before he fell into a severe sneezing and coughing fit. He rolled his tongue back inside his mouth, but this only made things worse. The boggart fell on the ground, his gray dreadlocks flailing as he sneezed and wheezed and rolled on the ground, scratching at his nose and mouth.

"Go!" Hoke shouted, squeezing Buttercake with his knees. "Fast as you can!"

Buttercake raced downhill, picking up speed, and Hoke clung tight to her neck. They shot invisibly past the drum circle, some of whom looked up at the mysterious breeze passing by.

Before she hit the flat land below the hill, Buttercake leaped into the air. The unicorn floated in a long, slow arc and landed well out in the plains. She jumped again, and they drifted over a farmhouse and a few low stone walls before landing.

With a third leap, they put the rocky hill of Glastonbury Tor, and its boggart guardian, far behind them.

"That's a good girl," Hoke said. "I don't suppose you've got a sniff of the magic instruments yet, have you?"

Buttercake neighed.

"That's all right," Hoke said. "Let's stop and swipe a few apples from the orchard up there, and you can sniff all you like."

As Buttercake walked, she drifted slightly to the west, as if she sensed something in that direction. Perhaps the instruments were somewhere near Exeter, or Plymouth, or across the sea in Ireland. Or perhaps the Americas, in which case Hoke hadn't picked the best gate to man-world, after all.

Hoke stroked her pink mane. Wherever the instruments were, Buttercake would root them out. Unicorns were good for much more than just running and hiding, though they excelled at those, too.

Chapter Nineteen

The sunlight was bright and thick on Sunday morning, and Jason woke slowly. He stretched, and then remembered all the things he needed to be panicking about.

Fortunately, everyone had been asleep when he'd slipped into the house. He'd made it to his room and slid his guitar under the bed without incident. But the real trouble would start today.

Before he even got out of bed, Jason dialed Mitch's cell number.

"Morning," Mitch said quietly, as if he didn't want to be overheard.

"So, how bad is it?" Jason said.

"Bad. House is wrecked, Mom's biting my head off. The neighbors told her I had a party, and she can see the place is destroyed, so..."

"Sorry."

"One good thing is that it really looks like an earthquake. It's too much damage, even for a wild party. The whole house is slanted now. The neighbors are all saying earthquake, which sounds impossible around here, but..."

"Why is that a good thing?"

"For the insurance," Mitch said. "I mean, if I tell them it was Dred's drum solo that did it, they'll just think I'm crazy anyway. So my mom's called the insurance company, and maybe they'll help pay for repairs. We don't know."

"That's good!"

"Well, we don't know anything yet. But obviously, that's it for band rehearsal here. My mom won't allow it, and I think one more song could blow the house down anyway. Your parents wouldn't let us rehearse over there, would they?"

"Yeah, sure," Jason said. "I'm not even supposed to be in the band anymore. Plus, you know, I don't really want my house destroyed, either."

"Maybe Erin or Dred's parents--"

"It could wreck their houses, too. We should probably work on figuring out how to not do that."

"Yeah, we'd run out of rehearsal spaces pretty quickly." Mitch was quiet for a minute. "But, you know, we really don't need to practice anymore."

"We don't?" Jason asked.

"Yeah, because those instruments are *magic*, man! That's our hook. That's what makes everyone go crazy for the music. Anything you play on those instruments sounds great."

"That's true..."

"So forget rehearsal. When Tadd gets this video ready, we'll put that out, we'll get gigs..."

"You're still thinking about the video?"

"Of course! That's our golden ticket. By the way, you need to go meet up with Tadd today. He wants to shoot some extra footage for the videos."

"Videos?" Jason asked. "More than one?"

"He says he's cutting a separate video for each song we played. Gives us more presence online."

"Okay. I don't know if I can get out today, though. I'm still in trouble with my parents."

"Tadd wants you to meet him at the Irvine Park Zoo," Mitch said.

"Why?"

"Extra footage, like I said. I'd go if I could, but I can't, because my mom would kill me if I said or did anything at all right now. And Dred's not even answering her phone, as usual."

"I don't want to ride all the way over to the park," Jason said. "It's hot out today."

"Erin's already there."

"I guess I should go, though," Jason said. "I mean, since you can't."

"That's the spirit. I'll tell Tadd you're on the way."

"Wait," Jason said, but Mitch had already hung up.

Jason got dressed quickly. He ran downstairs, then ran back upstairs, brushed his teeth and applied deodorant. Then he ran back downstairs.

His mom was at the kitchen table, painting some ceramic dishes while Katie watched, asking a million questions: "Why are you making that red? Isn't that too dark? Can I paint one now?"

"Hi, Mom." Jason drank a quick cup of orange juice, grimacing as it mingled with the lingering taste of toothpaste.

"You look like you're in a hurry," she said.

"Yeah...I have to go to the zoo. Just for a minute?"

"The zoo?" His mom scowled and shook her head. "You're still grounded. You can't go running around town with your little friends."

"I want to go to the zoo!" Katie said, and Jason saw his chance.

"Yeah, I'm taking Katie," he said. "That's what I meant."

"Yay!" Katie said.

"You want to take your sister to the zoo?" She blocked Katie from sticking her fingers into the tray of wet paints. "Stop it, Katie!"

"We could go now," Jason said.

"Yes, go! Katie, go to the zoo with your brother!"

"Yay!" Katie jumped to her feet. "Can we see the cats? And the monkeys?"

"You betcha." He beamed at her—saved by his little sister.

He ran upstairs and grabbed his guitar case, then ushered Katie towards the garage door. Unfortunately, his mom looked up.

"What's that guitar for?" she asked.

"For the animals!" Katie volunteered.

"Yep," Jason said. "We're going to play music for the monkeys."

"And the tigers," Katie added. "Tigers like guitar."

"Whatever." Their mom turned back to her painting.

They stepped into the garage and grabbed their bikes. He wasn't wild about Katie being around to embarrass him, but at least she'd gotten him out of the house.

"You're actually a pretty cool sister sometimes," Jason said.

"Sometimes?" Katie rolled her eyes and pedaled out into the driveway.

They rode their bikes across town, Jason keeping himself

between Katie and the occasional passing car.

They reached Irvine Park and pedaled back to the zoo area. They reached the long building where the monkeys lived, and Katie insisted on stopping to look at the family of white-faced capuchins. The adults rested quietly on their perches, while two little monkeys chased each other up and down the tree at the center of the cage.

Up ahead, he could see Tadd shooting video of Erin while she walked in front of the glass wall of the bear habitat.

"There's your girlfriend!" Katie pointed at Erin, shouting loud enough to get Erin and Tadd's attention.

"She's not my girlfriend. Just be cool," Jason whispered. Katie skipped along beside him as he joined them in front of the black bears. "Hey, what's up?" he asked, louder.

"Nothing!" Tadd complained. "I wanted *bears*. You know, primal, aggressive. Look at these guys. It's like the Berenstain Bears go to the beach."

Jason looked at the black bears. All of them were either lounging in the shade under the rocky cliff at the back of the enclosure, or lounging in the pond at the middle of it. One rubbed its behind on a tree, while another lazily scratched an armpit.

"I think they're fine like that," Erin said.

"We need to stir them up," Tadd said.

"Don't bother the bears!" Erin told him.

"Yeah, they're having a good time," Jason said.

"What else can we do?" Tadd asked.

"I'm Katie!" Katie announced to Tadd.

"Sorry, yeah, this is my sister," Jason said. "Anyway, you're the director, Tadd. What do you want?"

"Walk around in front of the bears. You and Erin together. Pretend you're friends."

"We are friends!" Erin said, and Jason had to swallow back the goofy smile that briefly spread across his face.

"Whatever," Tadd said. "We need different, like, emotion-images for different songs. So act like friends this time. You'll see where I'm going with this."

"Are we making a movie?" Katie asked. "Can I be the monster?"

"There's no monster," Jason said. "You can help Tadd direct."

"What's that mean?"

"The director is the person in charge."

"I can do that!" Katie walked up to Tadd. "Point the camera at them."

"I know!" Tadd said. He pointed the camera at them.

Jason set his guitar case on a bench and joined Erin at one side of the bear habitat.

"Do we talk, or what?" Erin asked Tadd.

"Yeah, sure. Like I said, friendly."

"What do we talk about?" Jason asked.

"Doesn't matter. It'll be music playing over it. Just pretend to talk."

"Okay." Erin shrugged.

They walked slowly in front of the bears. Jason did an exaggerated pretense of talking and waving his hands around, and Erin laughed and copied him, making fake silent dialogue back. They walked past the bear pond, to the end of the enclosure.

"This is boring," Tadd said. "Let's go see what the tigers are doing."

They walked over to the glass wall of the sandstone tiger habitat. The tigers were sleeping on the rocks, looking even lazier than the bears.

"Cats are the same everywhere," Erin said.

"Okay," Tadd said. "Now act like you're in love."

"What?" Jason asked.

"I have to show you in love so we can show you broken up later," Tadd said.

"Which song is this for?" Erin asked.

"Haven't decided yet."

Erin looked at Jason. "If you don't want to, maybe Zach's awake by now, and I could call--"

"I'll do it," Jason said. "Love and tigers. Got it."

While Tadd filmed them, Erin looked up into Jason's eyes, and Jason couldn't look away from her. She stepped closer and wrapped her arms around his waist. Jason hugged her, feeling awkward and dangerously excited at the same time. She leaned her head against his chest and actually sighed a little, and this made him relax and hug her close to him.

"Jason, you look off at the exciting, ferocious tigers," Tadd said. "Like you have something else on your mind. Like there's a tiger in you that wants to get out."

"Um, okay." Jason looked at the closest tiger, sprawled on its back on a boulder with its paws in the air. The tiger opened one eye, looked Jason over, then closed its eye again, completely not interested.

"Just hold that pose for a minute..." Tadd said, backing away.

Jason could have held it for hours.

"Good enough," Tadd said. "If only we could make these animals do something."

"Maybe they'll like some music." Erin took out her harmonica.

"Try it," Tadd said. He looked at Jason. "You really got those from elves, huh?"

"Fairies," Jason said. "How did you know?"

"Mick told me about it before the party."

"You mean Mitch?" Jason asked. "And you believed him?"

"No, I thought he was a total psycho, until I saw what the instruments could do. Then magic suddenly became the logical explanation."

Erin played an upbeat song on the harmonica. The tigers opened their eyes and lifted their heads. The closest one rolled over onto its feet and perched on top of the boulder, cocking its head as it listened.

"That's actually working!" Tadd said, raising the camera toward the tigers.

"Jason, grab your guitar," Erin said, and then she resumed playing.

Jason brought out the guitar and strummed along with her.

The two tigers jumped down to the ground and approached the clear wall as if entranced. They walked as close as they could, until their faces nuzzled the glass.

Jason kicked up the tempo. One of the tigers turned and gave the other a light swat. The second tiger jumped, then pounced, but the first tiger dodged. They scrambled after each other like playful kittens, leaping onto the boulders and then knocking each other off.

"Perfect!" Tadd said. "Now put your instruments down and pretend you're fighting."

"Like with fists?" Erin asked. She punched Jason in the arm.

"No, like an argument."

Jason put his guitar aside and walked up to Erin. She ran her mouth as if she were yelling at him, and then started poking him with her finger, as if accusing him of something.

Jason moved his mouth, pretending to yell back, and pointed back at her. Erin moved in closer, poking him more, staring him in the eyes with a look of mock anger on her face. Jason tried to look even angrier, and open his mouth even wider, as if he were yelling louder.

Erin stepped on his foot and stuck out her tongue at him, and then they both started laughing.

"No laughing!" Tadd said.

"No smiling!" Katie added. "You're 'pose to be mad."

"Yes, ma'am," Erin said. She made a snarling expression and pretended to yell at Jason again, and Jason jutted out his lower teeth and narrowed his eyes while he pretended to yell back. Erin put her hands on her cheeks and pulled down the skin on her face so her eyes were completely white, then she stuck her tongue out again, and Jason and Katie both laughed.

"Forget it, that's good enough." Tadd said. "Now the break up. Erin, turn your back on him and walk toward the camera. Create some distance. Look angry. Good. Now, Jason, watch after her sadly...good enough...and slowly turn back and face the tigers. Cross your arms. Perfect..." Tadd lowered the camera and looked around. "What else can we do while we're here? The cougars?"

"Hey, Tadd," Jason said. "Why don't you go film Katie running around the playground or something?"

"A solitary child, on a swing," Tadd said. "That's deep, Jason. Good thinking." He tapped his head, then pointed at Jason.

"I want to do the slide!" Katie ran up the hill. "Show me on the slide."

"She's an improviser," Tadd said. "That's good. Yeah, childhood memories...nostalgia...loss..." He followed Katie away up the path.

Jason and Erin looked at each other.

"So..." Jason said. "I think he'll make some good videos. You?"

"He's nuts. Why did we pick him again?"

"He has a good camera," Jason said, and Erin laughed.

There was a little silence between them. Erin watched the tigers, who slowed down now, without the music to inspire them.

"It's pretty hot," Jason said.

"Yeah."

"Want to go to the cave?"

"Okay! That sounds really good right now."

They walked down toward the woodland area beyond the bear habitat and into the mouth of a wide, cool cave with deep shadows.

There was standing water all over the floor, so they followed the stepping stones all the way to the back, where a narrow shaft of sunlight fell from a rocky chimney overhead.

"This might be my favorite place in the whole town," Erin said.

"Me, too. You know, the Leinenkugel brewery used to store their beer down here. Like a refrigerator."

"Yeah, everybody knows that," Erin said. "But I heard it wasn't really true."

"Maybe it's just one of those things everybody says."

"Just one of those things." Erin looked up at the light and closed her eyes. Her face looked golden.

"Erin," Jason said. He hesitated, then pushed on. "So, is Zach moving out of town. Like ever?"

"Why?"

"I don't know. He graduated. Is he just going to stick around and hang out with high school kids forever?"

Erin laughed. "He's waiting for me to graduate. Then he says we'll get a place in the Cities, or maybe even Chicago."

"Is that what you want to do?"

"I kind of want to go to Madison for college." She shrugged. "I'll figure it out. There's time."

Jason looked away for a minute, and then he worked up the nerve to say what he was thinking.

"I was thinking we could get dinner together," he said.

"Today?"

"Tonight. Or tomorrow night. Or...Over at Duncan Creek? What do you think?"

"Ooh, that's too pricey," Erin said.

"It's okay. Cashiers at Buddy McSlawburger's make the big bank. Actually, we're not even cashiers, we're 'Customer Happiness Engineers.'"

Erin laughed, then gave him a long look. "Duncan Creek? You're asking me on a date, aren't you?"

"Yeah. Or I could take you for fried cheese curds at the Fill-Inn Station, but I thought this would be nicer."

She laughed again, blushing crimson, which actually made his heart feel warmer inside his shirt.

"So, you're saying yes," Jason said.

"Jason! I have a boyfriend. I can't go on dates with other guys. What would Zach think?"

Jason couldn't imagine caring about anything in world less than he cared about Zach's opinion.

"You've been dating him since you were a freshman," Jason said. "Nobody else ever gets a chance."

"Right, cause so many guys are lining up at my door."

"I'm trying to," he said.

She smiled again. "Jason, I can't. I don't want to be one of those girls who cheats on their boyfriends, you know?"

"Right," Jason said.

They both looked around the cave for a minute, avoiding each other's eyes. As her rejection sunk in, Jason had a strange feeling, like someone had pounded his insides with a large hammer. He didn't want her to see how miserable he'd just become.

"So, I guess we should get back?" Jason asked. "They're probably done by now."

They followed the stepping stones out into sunlight, and then they joined up with Tadd and Katie. Tadd was now taking video of Katie doing a monkey-style dance in front of the capuchins. He lowered the camera when Jason and Erin approached.

"I wasn't done yet!" Katie shouted.

"Where have you two been?" Tadd asked. He raised the camera and peered at them through it. "Off in the woods together? Spill, we need it for the behind-the-scenes documentary."

"I should probably go," Erin said. "I need to get home."

"Yeah, me too," Jason said.

"Cool, cool." Tadd turned off the camera. "Think I got plenty of stuff here. Should texture up the vids."

"Thanks, Tadd," Jason said.

"Yeah, thanks," Erin added. She gave Jason a quick hug. "Bye, Jason. Bye, Tadd. Bye, Katie."

"Bye, Jason's girlfriend!" Katie sang out, looking back from the monkeys.

"Relax, Katie," Jason said. "She's definitely not my girlfriend."

Erin looked back at him, and Jason thought her eyes might have looked just a little sad. Then she walked out of sight along the path, heading for the bike racks at the front of the park.

"Come on, Katie, let's go," Jason said.

"Can we go to The Creamery?" Katie asked.

"No."

"Why not?" she pouted.

Jason thought about it. He certainly didn't need to save his money, since he wouldn't be taking Erin to dinner.

"You know, ice cream might be a good idea," he said.

"Yay!" Katie hurried up the path. Jason trudged after her.

"Yo, Jayce!" Tadd called after him. Jason turned back, and Tadd squinted one eye, made a gun with his fingers, and fired off a shot. "Nice shooting you."

"Yeah, I know," Jason said. "Everybody's shooting me today."

He followed after Katie, who was already way ahead, running through the arcing streams of water at the fountain, which was only as deep as a puddle, past other kids who were splashing each other.

He watched Erin ride out of sight, and then he ran to catch up with Katie.

Chapter Twenty

When he got home, Jason spent most of the evening in his room, listening to music on his headphones, but nothing sounded good to him. He felt stupid, and hurt, and stupid for letting himself get hurt.

Much later, close to midnight, he was awoken by a scratching sound under his bed. He leaned over, lifted the comforter, and looked underneath.

It was Grizlemor, arranging a small, straw-stuffed pillowcase and a rough burlap blanket in the space below the bed. There was also a rickety three-legged table with a wind-up alarm clock, and a lamp where a firefly orbited above tiny leaves and flowers.

"What are you doing?" Jason whispered.

"Just arranging my new place," Grizlemor replied. "What do you think? Not much of a view, but it's roomy."

"Your new...What? You can't live under my bed! And why would you want to?"

"Well, young sir, I can't live at home any more, and it's all on account of you. So, by any measure of justice, it's your job to provide suitable lodging during my displacement."

"Why can't you go home?"

"Queensguard." Grizlemor lay on one elbow on his blanket. "They're searching Goblin Row. I came home to find them ransacking my apartment pit. Had to run before they spotted me. I can only hope they didn't find my stash-hole."

"Why were they doing that?"

"Because of you!" Grizlemor snapped. "The Queensguard's mad as hornets about finding those stolen instruments. Magic leaking into the human world, and all of that. It violates the Supreme Law."

"What, the Constitution?"

"Not *human* law. Are you dense? The Supreme Law. The great covenant among the Folk, when we left man-world after the Iron Wars."

"I don't know what you're talking about."

"Human and Folk—that's us, goblins and fairies and elves and such—had a terrible war long ago. Your side won. So when we left your world, the Supreme Law was established by leaders of each kind of Folk. Rule one: Draw no attention from man-world. That means keeping all magic over on our side, hidden from your kind. Of course, rule two is that Folk shall not use iron against other Folk, yet there's the Queensguard, threatening everyone with their iron swords."

"Oh. But you didn't break the law, I did."

"As if it matters!" Grizlemor's green face looked agitated. "I led a man-whelp down to Faerie. It no longer matters whether the instruments are recovered—the Queen will punish me. Perhaps she'll throw me in the Labyrinth to be torn apart by beasts." He shuddered.

"You don't have anywhere else to go?"

"Don't even try to run me off," Grizlemor said. "It's too late for me to make amends, so now I have to make sure you don't get caught. It'll be my hide tacked to the palace wall if they find you."

"I'm sorry," Jason said. He wasn't sure he liked the idea of a goblin living in his room, but Grizlemor's troubles really were Jason's fault. "Are you sure you want to stay down there?"

"I like it very much." Grizlemor fluffed the straw pillow and lay back against it, crossing his legs. He took up a small leather-bound book and a tiny pair of half-glasses that looked like they'd been swiped from a grandma doll somewhere. He wore them low on his nose. "Now, if you'll leave me to my reading..."

"Wait. I need to know how the instruments work."

"Not being a musician, I wouldn't know," Grizlemor said.

"But you know some things. You know they drain energy from kids, and you said that helps power the magic in the fairy world."

Grizlemor sighed and looked up from his book. "What do you want to know? I'll share what little bits of knowledge I have, if it'll help you avoid trouble."

"Where do the kids come from? How do they end up in Faerie?"

"Fairy rings," Grizlemor said. "Remember the ring of mushrooms within which the young people dance?"

"Yes..."

"Here in man-world, such rings grow around the edges of soft spots between the worlds. Man-whelps can be lured into them by the faintest notes of fairy music. Once inside the ring, they fall through into the Faerie."

"So they're doorways. Like the one we used."

"Not exactly." Grizlemor sighed again, as if he found it ridiculous that Jason didn't already know these things. "A soft spot with a fairy ring is like a fishing net cast by the fairies. It's meant to lure people in. Fairies can create and remove them at will, with their magic. But they can't close the major doorways between our worlds, because those are holes that were left when the Folk cut their favorite places out of this world and moved them down to the elfland."

"You mean fairy-land, right? Faerie?"

"Let's not get off on a historical tangent," Grizlemor said. "It was the elfland then, but it's fairy-land now."

"I don't get it," Jason said.

"Do you want to know about the instruments or not?" Grizlemor was looking impatient, tapping his book with a green thumb.

"Yeah, tell me about those."

"As we were saying, the fairies create and control the soft spots. Their purpose is to trap human children so they can be drained of energy. The soft spot takes them directly to one of the little music parks in Faerie. There, in my world, the ring of mushrooms acts as a barrier—the human pups can't just wander outside the dancing-circle and do as they please. Not that they often try. They notice very little but the music."

"And when they're drained, they go back where they came from?"

"Correct," Grizlemor said. "Usually. They may pop up in a fairy ring in the wrong part of man-world, but back to man-world they go, in any case."

"That doesn't seem right, trapping and draining people like that."

Grizlemor snorted. "As if you aren't doing the same with your music."

Jason didn't know what to make of that, so he asked, "Grizlemor, the music almost destroyed my friend's house. How can we stop the instruments from being destructive?"

"Don't play them." Grizlemor began leafing through his book, as if he'd lost his place.

"Other than that."

"How should I know? It takes seventy-seven years of conservatory training before the Guild certifies you as a professional musician. I've had...let me consider...zero years of such training."

"But we don't want to wreck everything each time we play."

"Then play softly, I suppose." Grizlemor shrugged. "I'd prefer you didn't play them at all. You'll only draw the fairies' attention. And they'll be quite vengeful."

"How vengeful?"

"Have you ever been pecked to death by a vulture? Or slowly eaten from the inside by slime-worms? Or ripped apart by a blunt-toothed brainbug?"

"No..."

"Well, you might be."

"Great."

"Ask yourself if fame and fortune are worth a horrible death for you and your friends," Grizlemor said. "I know it's a difficult question."

"Are the fairies really that evil?"

"Evil? You're the thief. You've brought this on yourself."

Jason thought about that.

"Now, if you don't mind, it's been a long day. I'd like a bit of pleasure reading before sleep."

"What are you reading?"

"*Gobbligan's Wake*. It's a stream of conscious meditation on the nature of goblinness. You wouldn't understand it." Grizlemor pulled the comforter down like a curtain, closing off Jason's view of him.

Jason lay back on his pillow.

"I've got a monster living under my bed," he said.

"Goblin," Grizlemor corrected. "'Monster' is an offensive term." There was a cracking sound, then something thunked into the underside of Jason's bed. Jason could feel his springs rattle at the impact.

"What are you doing?" Jason asked.

"Clipping my toenails." Another crack, another thunk that rattled the bed. "Problem?"

"No." Jason listened, his lip curling a little as the goblin's next toenail clipping buried itself like an arrow into the boxspring. And the next. And the next.

Chapter Twenty-One

Tuesday afternoon, Jason was getting ready for another exciting day at Buddy McSlawburger's when he got the call from Mitch.

"You have to check it out," Mitch said. "It looks so good. I posted the link on your Facebook wall."

"The video?" Jason asked, running to his computer. His computer was running sluggishly, so it took forever for the video to load.

Over the phone, Jason could hear the current #1 hit song in America:

Alllllll day
And all night, too,
You dream of me
Yeah, you know you do…

"Are you listening to Claudia Lafayette?" Jason asked.

"No!" The volume turned down until Jason couldn't hear the song anymore.

"You were!" Jason said. "It's that stupid 'You Love Me' song."

"It just came on the TV. It's off now."

"Right."

"Are you looking at the video yet or not?" Mitch snapped.

"Oh, it's starting to load."

The opening credits appeared over Jason playing "Learning to Fly":

starring the Assorted Zebras:
Jason Becker
Erin Kavanagh
Mitch Schneidowski
Dred Zweig

Then those words disappeared, to be replaced by the words:

DIRECTED BY
TADD GRUBER

"It's epic," Mitch said. "Tadd sliced it into a different video for each song. You have to watch the last one, though. The cops coming in and dancing instead of busting the party. Dred's drum set transforming. The house shaking down all around the crowd."

Jason skipped to the final video in the series. The recorded music entranced him again—not as powerfully as playing the instruments live, but the effect was very strong.

"It looks like we spent a million dollars on special effects," Jason said, watching the walls crack and the windows shatter behind Dred, while her drums morphed into fairy drums.

"Right?" Mitch said. "And look at the pageviews."

According to YouTube, the video had been watched over 200,000 timessince it was uploaded at 6 AM. Jason glanced back at his Facebook page. Hundreds of people had "liked" the video, and it seemed like half the school had shared it on their pages. Jason had also been tagged in a number of videos uploaded from people's phones, showing the event from different angles, and those videos were getting a lot of views too.

On top of this, the Assorted Zebras page had six thousand fans, and Jason himself had hundreds of new friend requests.

"This is crazy!" Jason said.

"It was that first video, the one the kid made," Mitch said. "It's got like ten million views now. Everybody's looking for more stuff from us. A couple bars in Madison already emailed to offer us a gig."

"Are you serious?"

"But I'm waiting for more offers. I think we can do better."

"Don't get too cocky..." Jason said.

"I'm not. I'm just sitting back and letting the universe provide."

"Right. Anyway, I have to get to work. Text me if anything happens."

"You don't have to sling burgers at Bloody McSlobberbooger's anymore," Mitch said. "We're gonna be huge, man! This is just the beginning."

"When we get from the beginning to the part where we're getting paid, then I'll quit McSlobberbooger's. Until then..." Jason shoved the uniform and ridiculous hat into his backpack. "It's slawburgers, hold the slaw, a thousand times a day."

"I don't think you're seeing the big picture here."

"I don't think you're seeing the small one. What's happening with your house? Are they going to fix it?"

"Claims adjuster was here yesterday—that's the person the insurance sends to investigate, I guess. He seemed mostly confused about how we managed to have a tiny earthquake in Chippewa."

"Are they going to help?"

"We still don't know. He took a bunch of pictures and said he'd be in touch. But I'm still in deep trouble for having that party. So worth it, though. Have you seen the videos yet?"

"I'm looking at them." Jason clicked on the video for "Remember." It alternated between Erin singing and Katie wandering alone on the playground, as if Katie was the childhood version of Erin. It was actually a powerfully sad video. "Tadd doesn't suck," Jason said.

"He might be a nut roll, but he knows what he's doing," Mitch said. "Of course, the magic music doesn't hurt."

"Have you told Erin about all this?"

"Yeah, she's all over her Facebook page answering comments about it."

"Oh."

"Maybe you should call her, though," Mitch said.

"I don't think so. I'm off to work. Keep me updated." Jason hung up.

The Buddy McSlawburger's was packed wall to wall with kids from school. They erupted in cheers when Jason entered, as if they'd all been waiting for him.

"Jason," Mona said, approaching him with a hard look in her eyes.

"Hey, sorry I'm late. My friend wouldn't get off the phone."

"You told me there was a CD. I've been searching the internet for two days."

"Oh. Um...I'm sure we'll get something together soon, okay? I'll have Mitch burn you one."

"For free?" She embraced him in a tight, uncomfortably long hug. "Thank you, Jason."

"Sure." He patted her back. "Long line, huh? I'd better get to work." He managed to disentangle from her embrace, even though she tried to cling to his arms, then his hands, as he pulled away. He attempted to make his way through the crowd to the EMPLOYEES ONLY door.

"You don't have to do that!" Mona said. "Why don't you sit at this table and sign autographs?"

"You want me to sign autographs?" Jason asked, with a tremendous amount of disbelief.

The crowd applauded.

She led Jason to the first dining booth, telling people "Move aside, move aside." The crowd tried to crush in around him.

"This is crazy," Jason said. "All we did was put up a video."

"A great video!" shouted a girl he didn't recognize.

"I've watched it a hundred times!" somebody else yelled.

"I've watched it a thousand!"

In a daze, Jason sat at the table. People had him autograph napkins, except for a few who'd brought either notebooks or printed images of him.

"Where did you get this?" Jason asked a teen girl who handed him a picture of himself.

"It's a screenshot from you playing 'First Road Out of Here.' I *loooooooove* that song!" she said. "You're the best guitarist ever. I couldn't believe it when Kelsey told me you worked at McSlobberbooger's!"

"Who's Kelsey!"

"I am!" shrieked another girl. "He said my name!"

"So, do you guys go to McDonell?" he asked. He didn't recognize them, but maybe they attended the Catholic high school instead of the public one.

"Yeah, but I'll transfer to Chi-High if you want me to!" the girl called Kelsey said.

"Uh, that's okay," Jason said. "Thanks, though."

Jason spent most of his shift signing autographs and talking to fans, some of whom had come from the town of Eau Claire just to see him. He was in a daze. He knew the music was good, and it was literally magical, but this was too much. It scared him. The first video, the one taken by Mitch's kid neighbor, had only been circulating for a week or so. The music wasn't just entrancing, it was addictive, and everybody who heard it seemed to lose their minds a little.

Mitch was absolutely right, he realized. This was only the beginning of what promised to be a very wild ride.

Over the next couple of days, he continued going to work, but Mona treated him like a celebrity. So did the kids who came from increasingly far away—Sheboygan, Oshkosh, even college students driving up from Madison. All of them asked when they were doing a concert or where to buy their music. Lots of them took pictures of themselves with Jason. One group showed up with full-print posters of the band, which a girl who worked in a copy shop had made. Jason signed it next to his own face.

Mitch called periodically with updates. They were getting bigger and bigger offers for larger and larger venues. Apparently, even nightclub and theater owners weren't immune to the power of the Assorted Zebras.

On Thursday, when Jason was again at work and not working, Mitch called again.

"Forget all those little clubs. We've been invited to play at the Spoon and Cherry Festival on Saturday night," Mitch said. His voice was awed.

"Are you serious?" Jason whispered. The festival showcased eight independent bands from around the region, at the Statue Garden in Minneapolis. "That's like ten thousand people!"

"They had an opening, so the coordinator dropped us in," Mitch said. "Apparently a bunch of people had emailed her our video--"

"But how is that possible? Auditions for that were four months ago."

"Well, she may have bumped some local Minneapolis band to make room for us. But anyway, not bad for a first gig!"

"Saturday night? Do we have time to get ready?"

"We don't *need* to get ready. We just need to get up on that stage and play. The instruments will do it all for us. I'll announce it on our Facebook page. And our YouTube profile."

"I'll announce it, too." Jason stood up and looked over the crowd. "Hey, everybody: Assorted Zebras are playing the Spoon and Cherry Festival this Saturday! Tell your friends!"

The entire place burst into cheers.

"I think they'll come," Jason said into the phone.

"They can't, it's already sold out," Mitch said. "We just want everyone to know we played the festival, so we'll get more shows out of this. Gotta go, I have to call Dred and Erin!" Mitch hung up.

Jason's heart dropped a little at Erin's name. They hadn't spoken since she rejected him. This was going to be awkward.

A balding fiftyish man in a tie elbowed his way into the restaurant. Mr. Humphley, the franchise owner. Jason stood up automatically when he entered.

"What in the blue heck is going on here?" Mr. Humphley demanded. "Where is Mona?"

"I'm right here!" She waved from the cash register.

"Where's your cashier?"

"I'm over here, sir," Jason said.

"What are you doing sitting at a table, kid?"

"Signing autographs, sir."

"Autographs?" Mr. Humphley glared around at the teenagers packing the restaurant.

"Isn't it great?" Mona asked. "He draws a huge crowd every night. He's the guitarist for the hottest band on Earth!"

"I don't care if he's Elvis Aaron Presley! If he's on my payroll, he works. He doesn't sit around on his fanny!" Mr. Humphley approached Jason, glaring. "Got that, kid? Back to work!"

"Most of these customers just came to see me," Jason said, and twenty teenagers shouted their agreement.

"This is a family restaurant!" Mr. Humphley said. "It's not a disco for teenyboppers!"

"What's a disco for teenyboppers?" Jason asked.

"Get back to work or get out of here!"

"Fine." Jason grabbed the slawburger hat from his table and threw it into the crowd, who screamed and tore it to shreds. "I'm so sick of saying 'hold the slaw.' Nobody likes the slaw. It tastes like shredded garbage. Why don't you just take the slaw off the menu?"

"You're fired!" Mr. Humphley barked. "Don't show your face in here again!"

Jason pulled off the red Buddy McSlawburger's apron, tossed it on the floor, and walked away through the cheering crowd, most of whom turned to follow him out.

"Isn't he amazing?" Mona sighed at the counter.

Chapter Twenty-Two

Jason left work on his bicycle, waving off the countless people who offered to give him rides. He was in no hurry to get home. A number of cars followed him until he turned away from the road, cutting across parking lots, then back yards, and then across a cow pasture and into the woods, to escape the horde of fans following him.

Finally alone in the woods, he rode slowly alongside a small creek. He was worried about how he would act around Erin now, and whether she would hate him or, worse, feel pity for him, like he was some clueless little kid.

On top of that, he had to worry about the goblin that wouldn't leave his room—Jason was constantly picking up after Grizlemor, who was a confirmed slob. And the goblin was a reminder that somewhere, there were fairies that would be very angry when they found Jason. He couldn't believe that the little people with the butterfly wings were really so dangerous, but Grizlemor seemed terrified of them.

He emerged from the woods a few streets from his house, free of his fans now. He stopped in his driveway and took out his phone.

"Yeah?" Mitch answered.

"I have to tell my parents about the concert," Jason said. "They won't want me to go."

"Why not? It's a major festival."

"I'm not even supposed to be in the band!"

"You can change their minds," Mitch said.

"How?"

"The music, man! Once they hear the music, they'll see how good it is, and then they'll let you go."

"Don't bet on it," Jason said.

"Just let the music convince them. You know it will."

Jason thought about it. "I don't really feel comfortable using fairy magic on my parents."

"Why not? You're using it on everyone else."

"But not to trick them..."

"Tricking them into coming to our shows. Giving us their money."

"Yeah, but that's different." Jason rubbed his head, staring at his front door. Inside, the lights were still on, even Katie's. Everyone was still awake. "They pay to hear good music, and they hear good music. Right?"

"Right. And when your parents hear it, they'll let you do whatever you want. 'Cause it's that good."

Jason thought of the hordes of fans who kept showing up at work. He couldn't imagine his parents acting that way.

"Erin did it," Mitch said.

"She did?"

"Even worked on her jerk of a stepdad, and you know how he is. You've got the magic, so use it. I don't want you backing out of the show over this."

"I won't," Jason said.

"Then do what you have to." Mitch hung up.

Jason sighed, parked his bike in the garage, and walked into the living room.

"Home a little early, aren't you, son?" his dad asked. He was in his recliner reading a Sports Illustrated, while Jason's mom watched *Crazy for Ceramics!* on the Home and Garden channel.

"I got fired," Jason said, sitting down on the couch.

"What?" Jason's dad dropped the *Sports Illustrated*. "How did that happen?"

"Did you mouth off to somebody?" his mom asked.

"It's hard to explain," Jason said.

"Were you late?" his dad asked. "Or did you goof up your work?"

"It's not that. We made this music video--"

"When you were supposed to be working?" Jason's mother gasped.

"Goofing off while on the clock." His dad shook his head, looking disappointed. "What did I tell you about all that music nonsense?"

"No, we didn't make the video at work," Jason said. "We made it a while ago. But Mitch put it on YouTube, and it's really popular now."

"Videos of yourself? Why in the world would you want to do that?" his mother asked. "Don't you know the internet is forever?"

"Um...so anyway, Mitch made this video...well, actually Tadd made the video...no, this girl from Mitch's neighborhood actually made the *first* video--"

"That doesn't matter," his dad said. "We want to know why you got fired."

"That's why I'm telling you about the video."

"Oh, goodness!" his mom said. "It's not...*inappropriate*, is it? You don't use swear words or anything?"

"No, we just play music. But it's really popular. It's been watched by a million people or more."

"They must not have enough to do with their time," his mom said. "These kids."

"It's...they like the music, Mom!" Jason said. "That's why so many people watch it. And they share it on Facebook and Twitter and that other one...MySpace...so everybody who sees it shares it with more and more people. And so many people just really like the music."

"Stop trying to change the subject," his dad said. "We want to know about your job."

"So a bunch of fans starting coming from all over to McSlob...McSlawburger's. And the assistant manager told me to just sit down and sign autographs. Then the owner came in and fired me for sitting there and signing autographs."

"Aha!" his dad said. "Goofing off on the clock."

"But I did what the assistant manager told me to do."

"Why would anyone want your autograph?" his mom asked.

"Because, I told you, the video's a crazy big hit. In fact...we got invited to play at The Spoon and Cherry Festival. The Minneapolis Sculpture Garden."

"Absolutely not!" his dad said.

"But Mitch already told them yes," Jason said. "I can't let the band down."

"You're grounded, you get fired from your job, and now you want to run around with those kids from that ridiculous band?" his dad shouted.

"Like that Erin Kavanagh girl," his mom said. "I don't trust her, with all that wild-colored hair."

"It's not ridiculous!" Jason said. "And Erin's not a bad person. Dad, they're paying us a thousand dollars each. For one night!"

"A thousand..." His dad's eyes went wide, but then he blinked and shook his head. "The money doesn't matter. It's the principle of the thing. We forbade you to go hanging around those bad kids, and you ignored us. And you got yourself fired."

"But I got a better job," Jason said. "If I worked at McSlob...the hamburger place all summer, every day, I wouldn't make a thousand dollars." Jason didn't mention that all the money might have to go to Mitch's mom to repair her house. There would be plenty of shows ahead, the way things were going.

"I don't see why they'd pay so much money," his dad said.

"Because everyone wants to see us! We're pretty good." Jason hesitated, then plunged forward. "You should watch some of the videos. Both of you."

"I don't need to see you making an idiot of yourself," his dad said.

"We worked pretty hard on the music, Dad," Jason said. "We've been practicing for a couple of months. I'd really like you to see it, even if it doesn't change your mind. Please?"

"Oh, George, maybe we should watch it," Jason's mom said. "If he's worked so hard on it."

His dad grunted. "Make it quick."

"I'll show you." Jason walked to the little computer table by the half-flight of steps that led up into the kitchen. He pulled up one of the videos--"First Road Out of Here"--and played it. He cranked up the speakers.

"That's too loud!" his dad said. "Turn it...down..."

Jason's parents gazed at the screen, mesmerized by the sound of the music flowing out.

"See?" Jason said. "People like it."

His parents slowly stood and walked toward the computer,

completely entranced.

"It's so sad," his mother said.

"It's beautiful! Touching!" Jason's father choked up, clutching his heart. Jason wasn't sure his dad had ever used words like that before.

"Yeah, so you see why I need to go play this concert, right?" Jason said. "Everyone wants to see us. Mom? Dad? Are you listening?"

His parents were drifting closer and closer to the computer speakers, paying him no attention. It was creepy.

Jason paused the video. "So, can I go and play Saturday night?"

"What happened to the music?" Jason's dad asked.

"I want to hear more!" his mom said. "Right now, Jason!"

"Then tell me I can go play at the show."

"Of course you can go and play." Jason's father dabbed at his eyes with his handkerchief. "The world shouldn't have to go without music like that."

"Okay...great!" Jason said. "Thanks!"

"Would you push 'Play'?" his mom snapped.

"Sorry!" Jason unpaused the video. "There you go."

He watched his parents swaying to the music. His dad put an arm around his mom, and they swayed slowly together.

"So...I'll go tell Mitch, then," Jason said.

They didn't reply. They didn't seem to hear him.

Jason shook his head and went upstairs.

"What's that music?" Katie asked as Jason passed her door. She was stretched out on her bed, reading *Darkwing Duck* comic books.

"It's nothing," Jason said.

"Nah-uh. That's your music! Everybody's talking about it."

"Oh, *everybody* is, huh?"

"Everybody on the innernet!"

"Wow. Okay, see you later, Katie." Jason walked into his room and closed the door. A new, funky smell had infused his room since Grizlemor moved in.

"I'm hungry!" the goblin said from under his bed.

Jason knelt and lifted the comforter. Grizlemor lay on his bed, looking up from his book. He was surrounded by dirty spoons and empty cans: Beanee Weenies, Spaghetti-o's, chili.

"Why don't you clean up a little?" Jason asked. He gathered the cans into the trash bag he'd left under his bed for exactly that purpose.

"Take the trash bag with you when you go get me more food," Grizlemor said. "It's getting full."

"With no help from you." Jason gathered up the sticky, dirty spoons. "Don't you have anywhere to live yet?"

"Sure do. Right here." Grizlemor patted the carpet. "Nice place, too. Smells a bit like humans, but I'm taking care of that."

"You really are," Jason said. He stood up.

"Don't forget my food!" Grizlemor said.

"What do you want now?"

"Saltine crackers, topped with grape jelly, cheese, and chocolate syrup."

"Are you kidding?" Jason asked.

"Goblins never kid about food."

Jason sighed. He took the dirty spoons downstairs and put them in the dishwasher. He glanced at his parents, who were both hunched over the computer screen, watching another video, their eyes glazed. He didn't bother trying to hide the bizarre crackers as he put them together for the goblin. His parents didn't even seem to know he was there. They were lost in the music.

In his room, he slid the plate under the bed. He heard Grizlemor gobble them down, and he was glad he didn't have to watch—the goblin's eating habits were the most disgusting he'd ever seen.

Jason took out his phone and looked at Erin's number, which had a snapshot of her smiling face beside it. He wanted to call her, but what could he say? She'd made her feelings perfectly clear.

He threw the phone aside and took out his guitar. His hands played how he felt, the lower three strings, filling the room with sadness.

Katie wandered in, drawn by the music. She sat at the foot of his bed and listened, and she gradually began to cry. Not sobbing or screaming like she usually did, but just slowly leaking tears from her eyes while she watched Jason play.

Chapter Twenty-Three

The instrument factory sang and chimed with some of the most beautiful sounds Aoide had ever heard. They bounced and echoed pleasantly from the brick walls, where the bricks were the assorted colors of a bag of gumdrops. Sunlight poured in from the skylights and the huge wrought-iron windows, all of which were open to catch the buttery breeze from the bakery next door.

Aoide and Rhodia followed Ladon, a male fairy with long green hair, a golden nose ring, and a serpent tattoo snaking up his neck. He had dragonfly-style wings.

"We've got everything you need," Ladon said. "Visit the luthiers up here--" He pointed to where several fairies carved the pieces of a violin, working with slow, painstaking care. One of them had a violin string stretched taut between tall, glowing geodes. She sang a single long note to vibrate the string while it soaked in the pulsing light of the magic stones. Much of the work took place behind a tapestry, where brightly colored smoke rolled out while the enchanters cast their secret spells.

Neus and Skezg, the faun and the ogre, dragged behind them, watching young apprentice fairies cast spells over raw boughs and limbs, recently cut from trees and still damp.

"There's one very small issue," Aoide said. "Our last instruments were stolen, so we don't exactly have the money saved up to buy new ones."

"How much do you have?"

"Not much," Aoide said.

"It's not a big deal," Rhodia added, giving Ladon her most cheerful smile. "We've been playing in the park near Goblin Row for a hundred years, so we get the musicians' stipend from the Queen. Plus, we get a lot of gigs."

"You want to buy four instruments on credit?" Ladon stopped walking and whirled around the face them. He wasn't grinning anymore. "All four?"

"That's okay, right?" Aoide smiled widely at him. "We're Guild musicians and everything."

"If you weren't Guild musicians, the security spells would not have allowed you through the door," Ladon said. "Guild musician or not, you can't buy anything without money. You'll have to talk to our finance department."

"Oh, certainly," Aoide said. "I'm sure everything will be fine."

Ladon almost glared at her. "This way," he said.

He led them away from the factory floor, up a spiraling wrought-iron staircase to a row of arched wooden doors on the second floor, each one of them a different color. A wrought-iron balcony ran in front of the doors, overlooking the fairy artisans below.

Ladon knocked on the red door, then opened it.

"Mr. Wimwinkle," Ladon said. "We have some poor musicians trying to get instruments with no money."

"That's not a very nice way to put it," Rhodia said, and Aoide elbowed her to be quiet.

"Best of luck," Ladon said icily, as he walked away.

"Good fortune to you, too!" Aoide called after him. Then she turned and looked into the office.

One wall of the office was full of pigeonholes. A gnome sat at the big desk, surrounded by stacks of scrolls, which he was sorting into the pigeonholes. From there, pigeons took the scrolls and flew up a chimney to deliver them around town.

The gnome wore a tall, cone-shaped red hat and a blue jacket. A nameplate on his desk read DWOBKIN WIMWINKLE. He stroked his long, white beard as he looked at Aoide, Rhodia, and Neus, as well as the big, orange-haired ogre squatting behind them.

"Well, I doubt this will take long," the gnome said. "Come in, ladies. And gentleman. The ogre will have to stay out there, of course, there's no room."

Skezg grunted and hunkered low to the floor.

Aoide, Rhodia and Neus entered and took the chairs facing the gnome. Wimwinkle arched his fingers in front of his lips and looked them over.

"What kind of loan do you need?" he asked.

"We need to replace our four instruments," Aoide said. "My lute, Rhodia's harp, Neus' pipes and Skezg's drum."

The gnome whistled.

"That's a lot of silver," he said. "What do you have for collateral?"

"Not much," Aoide said. "The Queensguard is holding our savings for, um, security while they search for our lost instruments. But we play at parties and clubs all over the city, and during the day we have the park by Goblin Row. So we have income."

"And the Queen pays you the usual stipend for musicians who entrance the man-whelps?" the gnome asked.

"Every month," Aoide said.

"But this month, you'll receive nothing," the gnome said.

"Unless we have our instruments," Neus said, blinking his goaty eyes.

"And would you please explain to me what happened to your last instruments?" Wimwinkle asked.

"They were stolen!" Rhodia said. "Can you imagine? What a horrible thing for someone to do!"

"How were they stolen?"

"From the park," Aoide said.

"You saw it happen?"

"No, we were having a drink at the cafe," Rhodia said. "Right across the street."

"And you left your instruments at the park?"

"We do it all the time!" Rhodia said. She put her face in her hands, and her pink wings wiggled. "Nobody ever bothers them."

"But this time, somebody stole them," the gnome said. "So you want us to extend you a loan to buy instruments, knowing that you carelessly leave instruments out in a park near Goblin Row, where anyone who comes along might steal them?"

"We won't do it anymore! We promise," Aoide said, and Rhodia and Neus nodded.

The gnome sighed and shook his head. "Given all you've told me, we couldn't possibly extend a loan for the full amount of the instruments. You'll need to come up with at least half, which I calculate to be..." He moved several beads on an abacus. "Five hundred silvers."

"Where are we going to get five hundred silver coins?" Rhodia gasped.

"If we don't have instruments, then we can't earn the money to pay for them," Aoide said.

"It's a real conundrum," the gnome agreed. "Happily, it is not *my* conundrum to solve. Have a lucky day."

"We're done?" Aoide asked. "Just like that?"

"Unless you have five hundred silvers, we have nothing left to discuss," the gnome said.

"But...can't we just rent them?" Rhodia asked. "We have somebody searching for ours. We only need these for a little while."

"Instruments cannot be rented!" the gnome gave Rhodia a stern look. "You should know that is against the rules of the Musicians' Guild. Each instrument adapts to its user. They cannot simply be passed from one player to another."

"But some instruments can adapt to new players," Aoide said.

"Take it up with the Guild," the gnome said, waving them away. "Again I say, have a lucky day."

"Have a lucky day," Aoide mumbled. She stood up, her eyes stinging. She missed her lute terribly. She missed playing music. "Come on, everyone."

They shambled out of the factory and down Queen Boulevard towards Goblin Row. Nobody spoke.

When they reached their usual park, Rhodia gasped. Another band had already moved in, fairies with flutes and bells and a banjo. A group of young humans danced inside the ring of mushrooms, their energy pouring out to recharge the magic of Faerie.

"That's our spot!" Rhodia said.

"We can't claim it if we don't have our gear," Neus said. "If we stop playing there, another band can take it. That's the law."

"Let's get a drink," Skezg grumbled.

They took a table at their usual cafe. A golden-haired fairy fluttered to their table and took their orders: rose nectar for Aoide, honeysuckle dew for Rhodia, thistle tea for Neus. Skezg ordered a cup of poison ivy broth.

"What are we going to do?" Rhodia asked. "We can't play, we lost our spot. That elf and his unicorn better come back with our instruments, or we're sunk."

"If I ever find that thief..." Neus made a fist. "Pop! Right in the nose holes."

"I have to pay rent soon," Aoide asked. "I don't know how I can make it."

"Guess what? They're hiring here!" the golden-haired fairy chirped as she delivered their four drinks in bell-shaped lilies. "All you need is a great attitude and a quick pair of wings! Oh, and the ability to work your tail off all day for practically nothing! Let me know if you want refills!" She fluttered away again.

Aoide put her elbow on the table and rested her hand in her chin.

"We don't get to play no more," Skezg grumbled.

"That's right. Everything depends on that crazy old elf," Aoide said.

They sat in silence for a few minutes. Then Aoide stood and walked inside the cafe building, up to the front counter, where the golden-haired fairy waved cheerfully.

"Can I have one of those job applications?" Aoide asked.

"Certainly!" the fairy chirped. She handed over a scroll.

"Mind if I borrow your quill-and-ink?" Aoide asked.

"As long as you don't carry it away! I hate when people steal my pen. It makes me violent!" the golden-haired fairy giggled.

"Thanks." Aoide picked up the long plume of the feather quill pen, dipped it in the little oyster-shell inkpot, and began to fill in the blank lines on the scroll.

Chapter Twenty-Four

On Saturday, Jason dressed in a black t-shirt and his most comfortable jeans and shoes. He spent an unusually long time checking his hair in the mirror. The largest crowd for which he'd ever performed was a crowd of one hundred, and that had been as an extra in the high school production of *The Crucible*. He couldn't imagine facing ten thousand people. It made him almost as nervous as the thought of seeing Erin again.

Grizlemor appeared next to him. The goblin removed his hat and smoothed his knotty, stringy hair, then spread his mouth open and inspected his dark yellow teeth and lumpy green gums in the mirror.

"What are you doing?" Jason asked.

"Getting ready for the show."

"What show?"

"Do you really think I'm going to let the four of you run off with those instruments unsupervised?" Grizlemor asked. "Somebody has to watch out for wicked fairies."

"I'm sure we'll be fine," Jason said.

"I'm sure you won't. If the fairies figure out what happened, they'll kill me. Then I'll haunt you."

"Very funny."

"It's not funny." Grizlemor sniffed his own armpit. "Clearly, you've never faced a goblin ghost. We can get pretty ugly after we die. Go grab me a snack, would you? Whipped cream and Spam on rye, please."

Jason looked the goblin over. His clothes and hat were filthy, and he gave off a smell like rotten sausages.

"Are you sure you don't want to bathe before you go?" Jason asked. "Or wash your clothes?" He couldn't recall the goblin doing either thing in the week he'd been living under Jason's bed.

"Nope. I'm ready." The goblin disappeared in a green puff. A row of green puffs appeared, leading away to Jason's bed. Grizlemor reappeared on the edge of the bed, next to Jason's guitar case. "I don't see any snacks yet." He held out an empty hand.

"Do you really have to come? How will I explain you to everyone else?"

"Same way you explained the magic instruments," Grizlemor said. "They seem happy with those, don't they? Tell them I come with the instruments."

"Like a roadie?"

"What's that?"

"Someone who helps load and unload the gear."

"Whatever you want to tell them." Grizlemor took off his shoes and sniffed between his green toes.

"Change your mind about the bath?"

"I think I'm good for another five or ten years," the goblin said. "Food, please."

Jason shook his head and went downstairs. He walked into the kitchen, feeling annoyed, but then he froze when he saw who was at the kitchen table.

Both his parents were there, having mugs of coffee. A third mug cooled on the table, untouched. Behind it sat a withered old woman with hair like a mat of gray cobwebs. Her eyes were very dark, her mouth a narrow gash. She wore a black silk scarf around her neck, and where it drooped, Jason could see that her neck was swaddled in discolored bandages under the scarf. She sat in a wheelchair that looked antique, made of dark, polished wood and brass wheels.

Jason gaped. He could guess who she was.

"Jason," his mother said. "This is Mrs. Dullahan."

Jason gaped a little more.

"Where are your manners?" Jason's mom asked.

"Oh! Uh, hi, Mrs. Dullahan." Jason's heart sank like a stone in a cold pond. She'd figured it out, he thought, and she was going to take back their instruments before they ever got to play a show.

"She has a few things to ask you," his dad said.

"Okay." Jason's throat knotted up. The lady was scary. The air felt unnaturally cold around her.

"You are the young man who came to my house," she said, and he recognized the harsh, scraping voice from the intercom.

"Yeah. I mean, yes. My mom told me I should help you with yard work. But you said you didn't want me to."

"It was unnecessary. Mortimer handles all my gardening and caretaking needs." Mrs. Dullahan pointed to the corner of the kitchen.

Jason jumped when he saw the tall, wraithlike man in the corner, dressed in a black suit. A black chauffeur's cap was pulled low, shading his eyes so they couldn't be seen at all. His face was gaunt, almost skeletal. Mortimer didn't move at all, just stood with his arms folded in front of him. Jason had no idea how he'd missed the man standing there. It was almost like Mortimer had been concealed by shadows, except it was a bright Saturday afternoon and the kitchen was flooded with sunlight, so there weren't any shadows.

"But he gave you the muffin basket, at least," Jason's mom said to Mrs. Dullahan.

"What muffin basket?" Mrs. Dullahan asked.

"Jason! You didn't give her the muffin basket?"

"She told me to go away!" Jason said.

"Nothing was said about a muffin basket," Mrs. Dullahan hissed. "I would have liked a muffin basket."

"What did you do with the muffin basket?" Jason's mom snapped.

"Uh...my friends and I ate it," Jason said.

"Jason!" His dad shook his head.

"We'll get you another muffin basket, Mrs. Dullahan," Jason's mom said.

"Thank you. Though I would prefer an assortment of cured meats and cheeses," Mrs. Dullahan replied. "And crackers."

"All right...I'm sure we can do something," Jason's mom said.

"The day of your uninvited visit to my home," Mrs. Dullahan said to Jason, "Did you depart when instructed to do so? Or did you linger and snoop?"

"I didn't snoop," Jason said. "I left. I went to band practice with my friends."

"Taking the muffin basket with you," Jason's mom added.

"Yes! Sorry! I didn't know the muffin basket was going to be such a huge deal."

"It's not the muffin basket itself, it's the principle of the muffin basket," Jason's mom said.

"Someone has been snooping around my house," Mrs. Dullahan said. "I returned from my trip to find some of my lawn decorations vandalized."

Jason thought of the little wooden squirrel he'd broken when he landed in her back yard. He kept quiet.

"Did you have a nice trip?" Jason's mom asked. "Where did you go?"

"It was a hunting trip." Mrs. Dullahan's dark eyes hadn't moved from Jason.

"Ooh, yah? What were you hunting?" Jason's dad asked her.

"Prey." Mrs. Dullahan's eyes continued boring into Jason, and he felt like squirming. "Did you, or did you not, enter my yard at any time?"

"No," Jason said, after a brief hesitation. Could she tell he was lying?

"Are you certain?" Her mouth pulled down at the corners as she stared unblinking at Jason.

"Yes...Yes, ma'am."

"You did not enter my property? Did not climb my wall?"

"No." Jason's voice came out quiet and squeaky.

"Do you know of anyone who has?" Mrs. Dullahan asked. "Have other juveniles discussed such a thing? Perhaps bragging, as juveniles do?"

Jason shook his head. "I guess I can...listen and see if I hear anything." His gaze shifted from Mrs. Dullahan to Mortimer. The tall, gaunt man hadn't moved a bit. He was like a mannequin. A Halloween decoration, maybe.

"I hope that you will." Mrs. Dullahan's voice was icy now. She seemed to be angry at him. Maybe she really did know he was lying. He felt transparent, exposed, and vulnerable.

"The crime went beyond vandalism," she said. "Four musical instruments were stolen. A lute. A harp. Pan pipes. A drum."

Jason felt very cold inside. His guts were knotting up.

"Have you heard of anyone with such instruments?" Mrs.

Dullahan asked.

"No..."

"I understand you are a music-maker," she said.

"A little bit."

"Jason plays the guitar," his mom said. "We're very proud."

That was a little weird, too, but his parents' attitude about the band had changed drastically since the music cast its spell on them.

"I don't really play it that much," Jason said.

"May I see this guitar?" Mrs. Dullahan asked.

"Oh, sure!" his dad said. "Jason, why don't you go grab it and play a little ditty for Mrs. Dullahan here? He's really good."

"Um...I'm sure she doesn't want to hear me play."

"I would be delighted," Mrs. Dullahan said, and her words sounded cold and frosty. She stared at Jason with her coal-black eyes. She didn't sound like someone who could ever be delighted by anything.

"Go on, don't be shy," Jason's mom said.

Jason sulked as he walked upstairs. Katie's door cracked open as he passed it.

"Is Mrs. Dullahan still here?" Katie whispered.

"Yes."

Katie closed her door in a hurry.

Jason walked into his room, to see Grizlemor standing on his bed, arms crossed, impatiently tapping one rotten leather shoe.

"Where are my snacks?" the goblin asked.

"Sh!" Jason closed the door. "Mrs. Dullahan is here," he whispered.

"A dullahan?" The goblin's mouth dropped open, his eyes bugged out, and his pointy green ears jutted out at either side of his head. He bounced on the bed, then jumped to the windowsill. "There's a dullahan in your house? I have to get out of here!"

"Quiet! It's just *Mrs.* Dullahan. The old lady from across town."

"She's the guardian of the gate, is what she is," Grizlemor whispered. "I'm cooked if the dullahan finds me out here, wandering man-world. She's supposed to keep Folk like me in Faerie!"

"Why do you call her *the* dullahan?"

"That's what she is!"

"She's looking for the instruments," Jason said.

"Oh, no, even the dullahan is searching? You can't let her see it!"

"I wasn't planning to." Jason brought his old Fender guitar out of the closet. "Wish me luck."

"May you find luck-clovers in your garden," Grizlemor whispered.

"Okay," Jason said.

He walked downstairs to the kitchen, where everyone watched him expectantly.

"Is this your only guitar?" Mrs. Dullahan asked, scrutinizing it with narrow eyes.

"Yep," Jason said.

"Go ahead, play us something," his dad said.

"He's very good," his mom said. "We're so proud of how hard he's worked."

Jason sat on a stool at the breakfast counter. He plucked out "Learning to Fly," but it was slow and hesitant. He'd grown accustomed to letting the magic guitar do all the work for him, and he'd never really been that great of a guitarist in the first place.

His parents frowned, looking confused.

"That will be enough," Mrs. Dullahan said before he was halfway through the song.

"He's much better than that," Jason's dad said. "Play a different song. Why don't you play one of the songs from that video--"

"I don't think she wants to hear anymore, Dad," Jason said.

"I've clearly heard everything you're going to tell me," Mrs. Dullahan said. "Mortimer."

The tall, gaunt man finally moved, though he didn't say a word, and he barely made a sound. He grasped the handles of Mrs. Dullahan's wheelchair.

"Good afternoon to you, Mr. and Mrs. Becker," she said, and Jason's parents stood up.

"It was so nice having you stop by, Mrs. Dullahan," his mother said. "Feel free to join us ladies at the Lutheran Church anytime."

"I'm not Lutheran," she growled. Mortimer turned her around and wheeled her to the front door. Jason's dad held the door while he pushed her out.

"That's okay!" Jason's mom called after her.

Jason noticed the time on the microwave. "The show! I have to get going."

"I hope you play better than you just did for Mrs. Dullahan," his dad said.

"Are you sure you don't want us to come, Jason?" his mom asked.

"Oh, no, I've got enough to stress about. Thanks, though." Jason hurried upstairs. He slid his guitar case out from under his bed. It held the fairy guitar.

"What happened with the dullahan?" Grizlemor asked.

"She's leaving."

A horn honked, and Jason looked out his window. Dred's rusty van was in his driveway, waiting for him. Mortimer had just wheeled Mrs. Dullahan past it, towards a windowless black van parked on the street.

"Wow, that's bad timing," Jason said. He opened the window. "Just wait!"

Mortimer stopped, and Mrs. Dullahan turned back to look. Dred laid on the horn again.

"We're running late for the show!" Mitch yelled out the passenger window.

Jason grunted in frustration. He closed the window as Dred blew the horn a third time. Why couldn't they just wait until Mrs. Dullahan left?

"We can't let the dullahan see me!" Grizlemor said.

"I know, I know." Jason found his school backpack in his closet and dumped out the notebooks and pencils. He held it open toward the goblin. "Get in here."

"Excuse me?"

Dred's horn blew yet again.

"Shut up!" Jason said. "Come on, we have to go."

Grizlemor sighed. He disappeared in a puff and reappeared inside the bag. Jason zipped it up, slung it over his shoulder, and picked up his guitar case again.

He dashed downstairs, yelled a goodbye to his parents, and then he was out the front door.

"Don't bang me around so much," Grizlemor complained inside the backpack.

"Sh!" Jason said.

"Come on, come on!" Mitch yelled from the rusty van.

Over at Mrs. Dullahan's van, Mortimer had opened the side door, and a wheelchair lift slowly unfolded to the ground. Mrs. Dullahan was watching Jason and his friends closely as Mortimer wheeled her onto the hydraulic platform.

"What are you waiting for?" Mitch slapped the side of the van. "Let's go, let's go."

Jason didn't want to open the rear door of the van and give Mrs. Dullahan a look at all the instruments inside. He opened the side door and saw Erin sitting in one of the two back seats. She smiled at him, and for a moment, he completely forgot what he was doing.

"Jason, did you miss the part where we're running really, really late?" Dred asked.

Jason shook his head. He glanced at Mrs. Dullahan again, who rose up as the platform lifted. Then he climbed in and slid his guitar case between the back seats, and dropped the backpack on the floor. He finally remembered to smile back at Erin.

"Close the door!" Dred said. She threw it in reverse and backed down his driveway while he hurried to slam the door.

"Who's that lady?" Erin asked.

"Mrs. Dullahan."

"What's she doing at your house?" Dred asked.

"Having coffee with my mom."

They pulled into the street. When Dred put it in drive, the side door of the black van closed. The black van immediately started following them. Mortimer must have already been in the driver's seat, though Jason couldn't tell for sure, because the windshield was tinted black. Jason was pretty sure that wasn't legal.

"Isn't this exciting?" Erin asked him. "Our first show, Jason!"

"Yeah, it's great," Jason said. He couldn't stop looking out the rear window at the noiseless black van that followed them like a shadow.

"I'm so nervous. Aren't you nervous?" Erin asked.

"Yeah, very nervous," Jason said. He looked at her and tried to smile through his fear. He'd expected Erin to be cold after she'd rejected him, or treat him like a freak. If anything, she was acting friendlier than usual to him. Maybe she felt sorry for him.

"Why is Mrs. Dullahan following us?" Dred asked.

"Is she going to the show?" Mitch asked.

"Didn't you tell me you snuck into the fairy world through a door in her yard?" Erin asked.

"Yeah, I did," Jason said. "She's the guardian of the gate. She's kind of supernatural, or something."

"A monster!" Grizlemor appeared in a puff of smoke next to Erin's feet.

"A monster!" Erin screamed, pulling away from him.

"No, not me," Grizlemor said. "The dullahan. I'm a goblin, not a monster."

"What's the difference?" Erin asked.

"Hmph." Grizlemor sat on the floor.

"Uh, Dred," Mitch said. "There's a little green man in your van."

"He's with me," Jason said. "He's okay."

"Why do you call her 'the' dullahan?" Erin asked.

"That's what she is. One of the most dangerous sort of darkfae," Grizlemor said.

"Dangerous sort of what?" Mitch asked.

"Some fairies are drawn to evil magic," Grizlemor said. "Fairies being power-hungry nutters. The more they use the evil magic, the more it twists them into monsters."

The black van stayed close behind them as they drove away from Jason's neighborhood. Now Erin was watching out the back window, too.

"Is this something we should worry about?" Erin asked.

"If she follows us all the way to Minneapolis, yes," Jason said.

"So, what's with the goblin?" Mitch asked Jason.

"He comes with the instruments."

"A 'roadie,'" Grizlemor said, winking at Jason. "That's the correct term, right?"

"Oh, cool, a built-in roadie," Mitch said. "Man, these instruments just get better and better."

Grizlemor rolled his eyes.

"So Mrs. Dullahan is an evil fairy," Dred said. "Awesome. What does she want with us?"

"She's trying to figure out who used the fairy doors she's supposed to guard," Grizlemor said. "Because *somebody* trampled around breaking things, not being cautious like me." He glared at Jason.

"So she's after Jason?" Erin looked alarmed. Weirdly, that made Jason feel better. For somebody who didn't want to date him, she really seemed worried about him.

"Mrs. Dullahan doesn't know it's me for sure," Jason said. "She only suspected me because my mom made me offer to do yard work for her. I don't think she actually saw me when I went in and out of the door."

"She didn't," Grizlemor said. "She was away on the Hunt.

That's why you were able to get in and out of Faerie without her stopping you."

"What Hunt?" Jason asked.

"It's a darkfae entertainment. You don't want to know more." Grizlemor shuddered. "That's one thing about the Queen hiring these monsters. Darkfae are dangerous, but they aren't the most diligent employees."

"I think she's turning away," Erin said.

Everybody looked back. The black van glided off down a narrow wooded lane, towards Mrs. Dullahan's house.

"She's going home," Jason sighed.

"So we're good?" Dred asked.

"I think so," Jason said.

Dred stepped on the accelerator. As they left town, Dred played some Prince over the stereo, and their mood began to lift.

Chapter Twenty-Five

A security guard stopped them at the parking area near the Sculpture Garden. The area was packed with vendor booths selling food and drinks, plus a row of Port-A-Poopers. People were everywhere, most of them Jason's age or slightly older.

"This lot's closed," the security guard told them, leaning in at Mitch's window.

"We're supposed to play tonight. We're the Assorted Zebras," Mitch said, pointing toward the stage that had been built for the event. Another band was playing there now, a dozen people using a wide assortment of bells and whistles. According to the banner hanging behind them, that was the band name, Bells and Whistles.

The security guard stepped away and spoke quietly into his walkie-talkie. After a minute, a second man arrived. He had long black hair and a turtleneck shirt, headphones with a big antenna and a built-in microphone, plus a clipboard thick with papers.

"Yes, I am Franco," he said, in some kind of European accent that wasn't quite French and wasn't quite Spanish. "I am ze stage manageur. You are ze Angry Zebras, yes?"

"The Assorted Zebras," Mitch corrected.

"Ah...you should be ze Angry Zebras. More passion! More fire!" Franco made a fist.

"We'll think about it," Dred said. "Can you tell me where to park?"

"I zaw your videos, no?" Franco said. "The music was, how do you say, *muy fantastique*." Franco kissed his fingertips at Mitch. "Ze use of *cinéma vérité* technique, ze destruction of suburbia...it was quite ze statement."

"I'll tell Tadd you said that," Mitch said. "Parking?"

"Zis parking area is all full," Franco said. "You are very late. You must park in ze alley across ze street. I will send ze stagehands to help with your gear."

"That won't be necessary." Grizlemor hopped up onto the middle console. He had changed his appearance a little, making his skin less green and more of a pinkish human color, and his pointy ears had shrunk, their tips tucked under his cap. "Whatever these guys can't carry, I can."

"Your friend," Franco said. "He is a dwarf, no?"

"A dwarf!" Grizlemor shouted. "I hate dwarves! I sneak up behind them and pull their pants down at public events! Dwarf, indeed. I'll make you a dwarf!"

"He prefers the word, um, 'midget,'" Erin said.

"Midget? Is midget not ze more offensive term?"

"He's a little odd," Jason said. "We'll be right back."

Dred drove across the street and parked in the alley. The four band members took everything they could carry, Erin and Jason helping with the keyboards and drums. Grizlemor stacked the remaining black instrument cases into a wobbly tower on top of himself, so that only his dirty leather shoes could be seen under them.

They walked across to the park, where Franco was waiting with his arms crossed, tapping his feet, checking his watch, doing everything he could to let them know they were taking too long.

"Right zis way," Franco said when they caught up with him. He showed them where to leave their instruments near the stage. People were everywhere—stagehands, security, musicians, electricians. A huge stage had been built overlooking the lawn around the Spoonbridge and Cherry sculpture, which was a giant spoon holding a giant cherry in the middle of a pond. The Garden was full of giant sculptures, but that one was the most famous.

"Ze hospitality tent is down here." Franco led them to a huge shaded tent with mesh walls, nodded at the security guard as they entered. Inside, the large tent had clusters of folding chairs where the bands were all lounging, cooled by electric fans. Franco led them to an unoccupied cluster of chairs near the back.

"Help yourselves to ze craft service table," Franco said. He indicated a picnic table piled high with Doritos, Snickers, boxes of Reese's Pieces, and rolled-up sandwiches cut into circles. A plastic tub of ice was filled with Red Bulls, Cokes and Yoo-hoos.

"Wow!" Mitch said, grabbing Doritos and Reese's Pieces on the way to a chair.

"I trust zis is to your liking?" Franco asked.

"It's awesome!" Mitch leaned back in his chair, while Dred swiped a bag of ranch Doritos from him and tore it open.

"Let us know if you need anything," Franco said as he walked away. "I will alert when it is time for your set-up."

"Thanks!" Jason said.

"How's everybody doing?" Mitch asked, in the general direction of the nearest band. They ignored him, though, and kept talking among themselves.

"This is so exciting!" Erin said. She flung her arms around Jason's waist, and Jason hugged her close. He couldn't help his feelings for her, even if they weren't exactly welcome. She hugged Mitch and Dred, too.

Soon, Erin's friends Parker and Kennedy arrived, chatting happily, and bustled Erin to a chair away from the group. They pulled up their own chairs and opened bags of cosmetics they'd brought with them.

"How do you want your eyes?" Kennedy asked.

"All I can think is, put some color all around them, like an old glam-rock thing," Erin said, grinning. "Just the eyes, though. I don't want my whole face looking like that."

"You'll need tons of glitter," Parker said, setting out tubes of it on the counter.

"Hey, Dred, want your make-up done?" Erin asked.

"Yeah, we have everything here!" Kennedy waved at the bags.

"Nope," Dred said. She tied on a kerchief printed with cartoony pink skulls. She wasn't wearing any makeup. Her baggy t-shirt, shorts and sandals were a contrast to Erin's thrift-store dress with its faded psychedelic floral print.

"It'll look great, I promise!" Parker said.

"Nah, I don't want it sweating all over me," Dred said, leaning back and propping her feet on another chair. "Nobody looks at the drummer, anyway. Erin's our front man."

"Where's Zach?" Kennedy asked.

"Is he here yet?" Parker asked.

Jason sank to a chair facing Mitch and Dred. He wasn't going to get in another word with Erin, with her friends hovering around her.

"He can't make it," Erin said. "He's starring in a commercial in Chicago. Uncle Otto's Authentic German Pizza."

"That's so hot," Parker said.

"Awww!" Kennedy squealed. "I bet he'll be sad he missed all this!"

Jason tried not to listen.

"Are you ready for this, Jason?" Mitch asked.

"Doesn't really matter, does it?" Jason said. "The instruments will take care of everything."

"Mitch and I were talking about the set list," Dred said. "We think it would be good to begin and end with cover songs, just to be safe."

"Safe?" Jason asked.

"People like songs they already know," Mitch said. "We'll do a couple of those songs we used to goof around with."

"Those don't always turn out well," Jason said.

"The instruments will know what to do," Mitch told him. "They're smart like that."

"That's why the dullahan is so eager to find them," Grizlemor said. He was sitting on the grassy ground, stuffing peanut M&M's into a rolled turkey sandwich. He took a big, crunchy bite and talked with his mouth full, spraying bits of sandwich and candy. "The fairies invest a lot of magic into their music."

"The dullahan is after our instruments?" Mitch asked.

"Oh, of course," Grizlemor said as he chewed. "Even if she doesn't return them to the Queen, she'll want them for her own nefarious purposes."

"What Queen?" Dred asked.

"The fairy queen," Jason said. "Let's not worry about it right now. I like the idea of doing the cover songs, that'll juice up the crowd. Let's do that."

"Good, we agree. Go tell Erin." Mitch opened a Yoo-Hoo and picked up a Snickers.

"If the chatterbrains will shut up for a second," Dred whispered.

Jason looked across the room at Erin. After a minute, Kennedy and Parker left for the bathroom, giggling and chatting with each other nonstop. Jason didn't know how they could hear each other, when neither of them ever stopped talking.

He approached Erin, who was checking her dark red lips in a cosmetic mirror. With all the glittering make-up, she looked almost like a different person, some model from a magazine.

"Erin?" he said. She smiled brightly at him in the mirror.

"Hi, Jason. Want to sit down?"

He took the chair beside her and told her Mitch and Dred's ideas about their set list.

"Sounds good to me," Erin said. She turned and looked him in the eyes. "Is there something else?"

"Yeah." Jason fidgeting in his chair while he reached into his jeans pocket. He took out a square of folded notebook paper. "You know I don't really write songs, right?"

"Right..."

"But this one I've kind of been working on. I thought you might like it, or you might take a look at it, or something. It's called 'Angel Sky.'"

"You wrote a song? That's really cool." She smiled at him, holding his eyes with hers, while her hands unfolded the page.

"You don't have to read it now or anything," Jason said.

"I want to." Erin looked at the page. As she read, her smile faded, and a serious look came over her face. She looked up at him. "Jason, is this--"

"There's our girl!" Kennedy said as she and Parker returned. They took up posts on either side of Erin, as if to block Jason from getting too close to her. Their endless conversation took over, and soon Jason moved back to join the rest of the band.

"Grizlemor was saying maybe we should go easy with the instruments, if we don't want to wreck any more buildings," Jason said.

The goblin, who hadn't stopped stuffing his face, gave a thumbs-up.

"We want to blow this crowd away, though," Mitch said.

"We don't have to try so hard," Jason said. "Just play kind of lightly. Let the magic do its thing."

"Sounds good to me," Dred said. "I don't want to make any more earthquakes, with all these people around. And I'd really hate to be the person who broke the Spoonbridge and Cherry."

They heard the sound of instruments tuning out on the stage, and then a huge crowd screaming.

"Who's the next act?" Jason asked.

"Programmed Chaos," Mitch said. "Some local band."

"They're great," Dred told him. "Their songs are like social and political criticism with an ironic pop overlay."

Jason shrugged. "Okay. Sounds good."

Eventually, Programmed Chaos began to play their first song, "The White House is Their House," which had gotten some attention from college radio stations across the Midwest, as well as NPR.

"Oh, Programmed Chaos!" Erin said, jumping up from her chair. Her friends followed her toward the stage.

"Their singer is so cute!" Kennedy said.

"He really is," Erin agreed. Then she stopped at the door. "Are you coming, Jason?"

"Me?"

"Yeah, let's go watch," Dred said as she stood up.

Jason caught up with Erin, while Dred and Mitch followed. The six of them left the room, leaving Grizlemor alone to wolf his way across the refreshment table. Mitch tried again to wave to the other bands, but nobody would look at them. Jason wondered if they resented how the coordinator had kicked out another band to make room for the Zebras, who hadn't even auditioned.

They stood to one side of the stage, watching the band. Erin and her two friends danced along with the music.

Jason looked out at the quiet, bored-looking audience of thousands, most of them teenagers. The show had sold out and the park was packed, but nobody seemed to be getting into the music.

Programmed Chaos, which consisted of three college-aged guys, finished their first song. They received sparse applause and scattered boos.

"Rough crowd," Mitch said.

The band went into their second song, and the whole crowd starting booing halfway through. By the third song, the crowd started chanting "Ze-bras! Ze-bras!" and stomping their feet.

"Oh no," Erin whispered. "I feel bad for them."

"I feel bad for us," Dred said. "We have to play for this audience, too."

The band hurried through another song while the crowd drowned out their music, chanting for the Assorted Zebras. The crowd pelted the band with lemonade cups, soft pretzels, and shoes.

"That's it!" the lead singer shouted into the microphone. "You want us gone, we're gone."

The crowd applauded and whistled.

Programmed Chaos hurriedly broke down their gear with the help of stagehands, then stalked off the stage, glaring at the Zebras.

"Stupid kids just want to hear you," the lead singer sneered at Erin.

"Yeah, way to ruin the gig for the rest of us. Thanks a lot," the band's DJ said. The three of them carried their equipment towards their small bus, and the lead singer went inside and slammed the door.

"Zis is an emergency!" Franco said, running up to them. He wore some kind of radio/microphone headset now. "You must play now!"

"That crowd's going to eat us alive," Erin said.

"Ze show must go on!" Franco said.

"Great," Mitch said, shaking his head.

All the overhead stage lights went out. In the dimmed footlights, a couple of stagehands helped them set up. Grizlemor quietly appeared and disappeared when the stagehands weren't looking, helping to bring out the pieces of the drum kits and the keyboard arrangement.

The crowd kept chanting "Ze-bras! Ze-bras!"

Jason looked out over the huge crowd, stunned by the sight of so many people eager to hear them play. Right now, he was a shadowy outline against the city lights of Minneapolis glittering behind the stage. In a few minutes, the big spotlights would come on, and he'd be looking at a sea of faces. And they'd all be looking back at him.

"What do you think?" Erin whispered beside him, looking over his shoulder.

"We'll just do our best," Jason said. "They'll like it or hate it."

"I am totally scared right now," she whispered. Jason took her hand, and she squeezed her fingers around his for a minute. Her cheek was next to his. She was close enough to kiss, but Jason resisted the temptation.

Erin stepped back and blew a few notes on her harmonica. A slight breeze crossed the stage.

Finally, Mitch and Dred announced they were ready. The band did a quick sound check, and as usual, the instruments were perfectly in tune with each other.

"We are ready to play, yes?" Franco asked. He touched a button on his headset. "Ladies and gentlemen...you have been chanting for zem all day...ze Assorted Zebras!"

Franco dashed out of sight as the curtain opened. Ten thousand audience members screamed and cheered. The wave of sound was so loud it seemed to push Jason backwards. He was overwhelmed by all the faces—but then the spotlights flicked on, and he couldn't see them anymore.

"Hello, Minneapolis!" Erin said into the mike, and she grinned from ear to ear when the crowd renewed its cheering.

Dred, Mitch and Jason started playing. Jason's guitar sounded electric now, as if it already knew what he was about to play.

Erin gazed out at the lights and the wild crowd. Then she sang the first verse of "I Love Rock and Roll" by Joan Jett and the Blackhearts.

The crowd erupted again, howling and clapping. Jason felt the guitar growing warm in his hands. The strings drew his fingers toward them like iron to a magnet. He barely had to concentrate. It was almost as if he were just an audience member, listening to the music as it happened.

Jason glanced around at Mitch and Dred. Both of them wore huge smiles, entranced by the music.

When they reached the end of the song, they stopped playing their instruments, but Erin spontaneously decided to sing the chorus one more time, a capella. It was just Erin's voice over the amplifiers, plus thousands of delirious audience members singing the words along with her.

When she finished, the crowd howled and cheered and stomped. She looked at Jason, and they shared glowing smiles.

From there, they played "Cinderella Night," since that was the first song that made them popular. Then they continued through all of Erin's songs. Jason could feel the audience turning somber, then sad, then cheerful, then ecstatic, reacting deeply to the music. His guitar grew hotter and hotter in his hands, and he found himself drifting towards the cool, damp air pouring out from Mitch's keyboards.

The audience grew crazier and more excited with every song. When they hit the end of Erin's list, she started a new song, apparently improvising the lyrics. Jason had never heard it before, but his guitar seemed to know just how to play it. It was a light, cheesy, nonsense song that didn't sound like anything Erin would write:

Everybody wave your hands!
Everybody shake your pants!
Everybody do it, do it, do it,
Everybody do the sugar dance!
The sugar dance! Yeah, yeah...
The sugar dance! Yeah, yeah...

The entire crowd danced together, suddenly synchronized as if they'd all practiced the dance together before coming to the show. It reminded Jason of that bizarre moment in any musical when suddenly everybody broke into song and choreographed dancing. He'd sometimes wondered what that would be like in real life, if you could just be at school or work and everybody stopped what they were doing to sing and dance together.

When she finished, the crowd roared so loud Jason thought he could feel the stage rumble beneath his feet. It was exhilarating. It was frightening.

The band members looked at each other, confused. Mitch covered his microphone with his hand.

"What the heck was that?" Mitch asked.

"I don't know," Erin said. "It just came to me."

"Can we just do the last song and get out of here?" Dred asked. "That crowd is freaking me out. Nobody should like us this much."

"Yeah, let's hit the finale and go," Mitch said.

Mitch played a synthesized sitar on his keyboard. Dred and Jason joined in, and then Erin sang the opening words for "Paint It Black," another song they'd toyed around with in Mitch's garage, though they'd never really played it very well. Jason thought it sounded amazing with a female vocalist, though, especially if that vocalist happened to be Erin.

For the first time, they played the song in perfect sync with each other, without a misstep. They reached the instrumental part, where Erin hummed instead of singing. Jason usually bungled this, but tonight it flowed like water, his fingers knowing exactly where to touch the strings.

Then the guitar seemed to take over, running away with him.

Jason couldn't stop playing, and the sound grew faster and louder and more complex all at once. The other instruments gradually faded and stopped as the band left him to his runaway guitar solo.

The air around him thrummed with power, as if all the energy put out by the crowd was flowing right to him. The guitar was searing hot in his hands now, and the strings burned his fingertips, but he couldn't stop playing. He wondered if this was how Dred felt just before the earthquake. He was afraid it might be.

The air shimmered and rippled like heat waves from the hood of a car. He was dripping with sweat, all of his clothes soaked, his socks squishing inside his shoes. And still his guitar grew hotter.

The heat waves thickened into a scorching bubble that surrounded him, distorting the whole world. Sweat poured into his eyes and the salt stung, but all he could do was close his eyes and keep playing.

Then, after what felt like years, he reached the end of his solo. His hands dropped away from the guitar, and he stumbled backwards, on the verge of a heat stroke.

He watched the thick bubble of rippling heat float up and away from the stage, out over the crowd. It was as tall as Jason himself.

The crowd was watching, too.

Jason stared, unable to look away, horrified that something terrible was about to happen.

When it floated above the center of the crowd, the huge heat bubble ignited, lighting up the entire audience like a blinding solar flare. Plumes of fire arced out in every direction. The flames billowed down toward the crowd—all of whom stood and watched, their mouths gaping open. Fire was about to rain down on everyone, and nobody was getting out of the way.

Jason wanted to grab the microphone, warn everybody of the danger, tell them to run, but he couldn't move. He felt like he was in a dream, one of the ones where a monster was chasing you, but your feet wouldn't budge.

Then the flames turned to a cloud of red smoke.

After a moment, the entire audience exploded in cheers, applause, stomping, screaming and howling. They surged toward the band, reaching out their arms. Jason and Erin, near the front of the stage, stumbled back from the roaring outburst. Erin stumbled and caught his arm, and he somehow kept her from falling. He wasn't sure how he hadn't fallen over himself.

"Is that it?" Erin whispered.

"I think we're done," Jason said.

Erin let go of his arm and walked back to the microphone.

"Thank you, Minneapolis!" she shouted, and the crowded roared back at her. "Good night!"

The four of them got offstage as fast as they could. In Jason's case, this meant a slow stagger, and he was the last one to escape into the wings.

He immediately peeled off his black t-shirt and tried to mop up his face with it, but the shirt itself was dripping sweat. A stagehand gave him a Spoon and Cherry Festival t-shirt, and Jason mopped what felt like a gallon of sweat from his hair, face, and neck.

"Wow," Erin was saying. "Wow."

"No kidding," Mitch said.

Dred was just shaking her head, a smile burned into her usually impassive face.

The audience's howling and screeching gradually fell into a steady pattern, a single repeated word echoing again and again through the theater: "En-core! En-core! En-core!"

"Oh, we can't," Jason said. He was out of breath and close to collapsing.

"Please, you must play one more," Franco said, arriving to meet them. "The crowd, zey will tear ze entire place apart wizzout an encore! And for me. I want to hear encore, too."

"We don't have any more songs," Dred said. "Unless Erin wants to make something up again."

"We could do another cover," Mitch suggested.

"Wait," Erin said. "We do have one more song." She gave Jason a sly smile. "Will you get the lyrics from the tent for me?"

"Oh, no, wait," Jason said. "We haven't practiced that one at all. I don't even know if it's ready. Or if it's any good."

"It's good," Erin said. "I like it."

"Really?" Jason blushed. "I kind of did work out something on the guitar for it..."

"Fine, you guys lead, I'll follow, whatever," Mitch said. "Let's just give this crowd something before they riot."

"Let's go," Dred said, jogging up the steps to the darkened stage. She looked eager to play more.

When they were on the stage, Erin took his hand.

"I want you close when I sing this," Erin whispered. "You'll do some of the vocals."

"I'm not any good at singing," he said.

"Maybe that's what you thought before," she said. The spotlights lit up again so the big crowd could see them, and the Sculpture Garden filled with cheers and screams. "But look. You're a rock star now."

Jason looked out at the mass of ecstatic people, and he couldn't help smiling.

"Do you guys want a little more?" Erin asked into the microphone. They roared back their assent. "How about a new song nobody's ever heard?" They cheered again. "This one is called 'Angel Sky.' It was written by our guitarist, Jason Becker."

Erin took Jason's hand and raised it high, and the crowd went wild.

"Hey, let's hear it for our drummer, Dred Zweig, too!" Erin said, and Dred tapped out a quick rhythm, to more applause. "And the guy who put this band together, our keyboardist, Mitch Schneidowski!"

"*Mick,*" Mitch said into his mic, but his voice was drowned under the tidal wave of screams and cheers. He looked out on the crowd, blushed crimson, and then waved. "Forget it."

"Jason, get us going," Erin said.

Jason started to play the guitar part he'd practiced for her song. It came out smoothly on the fairy guitar, not hesitant or choppy at all. He repeated the opening a few times, letting Erin and the others hear it and get used to it.

Instead of singing, Erin spoke into the microphone again.

"You know how the sky looks when a storm is over?" she asked. "Those golden beams of light ripping up the dark clouds? My grandmother told me that was the angels coming back to chase away the darkness. She called it an angel sky." She turned from the audience to look at Jason, but she kept her mouth by the microphone. "I told Jason about it before rehearsal one day, when a storm had just ended. I showed it to him. I guess he was listening."

Jason gave her a smile.

He played the opening again, and Erin sang:

After the storm,
You bring the light
I saw the angel sky

In your green eyes...

Jason's guitar knew just how to play the song. This time, the guitar wasn't overpowering him—he was putting himself into the instrument.

The rest of the band joined in softly. Jason sang the chorus parts along with her.

By the end of the song, half the audience was in tears, and half of them were kissing each other.

"Thank you, Minneapolis," Erin whispered again into the mic. She was crying, too. "Good-bye."

They left the stage to softer, gentler applause.

Chapter Twenty-Six

"Ze coordinator is horrified about ze pyrotechnics," Franco said in the hospitality tent. Everyone was relaxing, having pops or Yoo-hoos. Grizlemor had hidden himself somewhere. He'd spent the show eating every morsel of food on the table. "But I tell her: no, zis was not planned...but yes, no one was harmed, and ze audience is going home happy."

"Yeah, sorry about that," Jason said. "We should have, uh, mentioned it was going to happen."

Franco looked at the stripped-bare refreshment table. "Do you require any additional hors d'oeuvres?"

"Anyone?" Mitch asked.

"I think we're good," Erin said. "Thanks."

"I should tell you, your music..." Franco began to weep. "Your music!" Franco bawled and threw his arms around Mitch, who stood near him. He cried into Mitch's shoulder.

"Uh, glad you like it," Mitch said, patting his arm and giving Jason a puzzled look.

"I am such a fraud!" Franco said. "In truth, I am from Joliet, Illinois. I am not European. But I have faked zis accent for zo long I cannot make it ztop!"

"Sorry to hear that, guy." Mitch tried to pull away, but Franco hugged him close, crying harder.

"I can no longer live a lie!" Franco said.

"It's okay, dude, seriously." Mitch pulled away.

Franco wiped his eyes and nose on the sleeve of his turtleneck.

"I apologize for ze strong reaction your music made in me," Franco said. "Zimply notify me when you are ready to depart for ze night, if you wish ze stagehands to assist. Thank you for such...ah! Magical music."

Grizlemor appeared in a puff between Jason and Erin's chairs. His green stomach was swollen to three times its usual size, bulging out between his shirt and his trousers.

"Why didn't you ask for more food?" the goblin demanded.

"Why didn't you leave some for other people?" Jason asked.

The goblin belched. "You eat what you can, when you can. That's my philosophy."

They hurried to pack up their instruments, feeling both exhausted and giddy.

They slipped across the street toward they alley where they'd parked, while the crowd was still stomping and demanding yet another Assorted Zebras encore. Grizlemor again carried a precariously tall stack of black instrument cases.

"Can you believe that crowd?" Mitch asked. "We're going to have every big music label knocking down our doors after that."

"This whole thing is out of control," Dred replied.

"In a good way," Jason said, but Dred just frowned.

As they approached her van, both of the back doors opened from the inside, but the van's interior lights remained dark. The five of them stopped in the middle of the alley, staring.

"Uh, Dred?" Erin asked. "Who's in your van?"

A small man, about three feet high, stepped out onto the van's back bumper. He had gray and black beard stubble, and he chewed what looked a piece of stiff pink straw. He wore a battered old gardening hat and a long horsehair coat over mud-stained leather boots. The coat was open, and Jason could see part of a belt with several drawstring pouches and a sheathed knife.

"Who are you?" Dred asked, putting her drum case down.

"I am Hokealussiplatytorpinquarnartnuppy Melaerasmussanatolinkarrutorpicus Darnathiopockettlenocbiliotroporiqqua Bellefrost." The little man hopped down to the asphalt, eyeballing the five of them like an old gunfighter.

"An elf!" Grizlemor whispered.

"I come on behalf of Her Majesty Queen Mab, Empress of Faerie, Conqueror of the Elflands," the elf said. "Not to mention some awfully sad-looking musicians. Buttercake here says you have the four instruments of high magic stolen from the realm of Faerie, which violates the Supreme Law and all of that."

"Our instruments are not stolen!" Dred said.

"They are kind of stolen," Jason whispered.

"What?" Mitch said. "You never told us that."

"I thought it was kind of obvious," Jason said.

"You will return the four instruments to me," the elf said. "Or Buttercake and I will be forced to take them from you."

Behind him, the smallest horse Jason had ever seen, even smaller than a miniature pony, jumped out of the van. It floated gently to the ground beside the tiny man. It had golden fur, a pink mane, and a pink horn the color of rock candy jutting from the center of its forehead. Its eyes were huge, the color of chocolate.

"He's got a unicorn!" Grizlemor squealed. He disappeared in a green puff, and the stack of equipment he'd been carrying crashed to the asphalt.

"Are you giving them up, or am I fighting you for 'em?" the elf asked.

"We'll return them when we're done," Jason said.

"When do you figure that might be?" the elf asked.

"Whenever we're done being rock stars," Mitch said.

"Which we haven't really started yet," Dred added.

"A day or two?" the elf asked.

"Maybe a few years?" Erin said. "Not forever."

"Years!" The elf spat on the ground. "You've got ten seconds."

"Maybe we should give them back," Jason suggested, but the other three told him to shut up.

"Three, two, and one," the elf said. "Last chance."

"We need these instruments," Mitch said.

"Guess you made your choice," the elf said. "Buttercake...go get 'em, girl."

The little unicorn pawed at the ground like a bull and lowered its head. It pointed its horn at each of them in turn.

"Okay," Erin said, "That is the cutest thing I've ever seen. I'm taking a picture." She took out her phone.

The unicorn charged. She grew larger with every step, turning into a full-size horse, and then a giant horse the size of rhinoceros.

Her pink horn grew into a long spike, and sharp barbs of horn curled out all over its surface.

A double row of pink spikes grew out through her mane and continued all the way down her back. Pink armor plates formed over her ribs and joints.

The huge, beastly unicorn opened its mouth and blew out a wide plume of fire. Its horn pointed right at Mitch as it charged.

"Not so cute!" Erin screamed.

Everyone backed away except Dred, who dropped to her knees by her drum case and flipped it open. She set the snare drum on the ground and pounded it with both fists.

The ground beneath them quaked, and shock waves rippled toward the unicorn, shattering asphalt and concrete like they were glass. Dred's van bounced up and down, and the elf was knocked flat on his back. He fought to regain his balance, but each time he tried to stand, another shock wave toppled him again.

The massive, armored unicorn kept charging forward against the shock waves, but she began to stumble and stagger back. She let out an annoyed snort, and then two huge flaps of skin peeled away from her sides. They formed into pink, leathery bat wings. She leaped into the air and climbed high above them in the alley, beating her wings and blowing another jet of fire.

Dred stopped playing. "Are you guys going to help?" she asked. "Mitch, make a little storm or something!"

"Uh, okay..." Mitch took the fairy keyboard from its case and knelt in front of it. The device took no electricity at all—it ran on some kind of magic. Mitch stretched his fingers above the keys, but then he hesitated.

Above them, the unicorn twisted in tight circles just above the alley. It was growing even larger, its body longer and snakelike, the pink armor plates sprouting everywhere. Its cloven hooves cracked, split and unfolded into thick pink talons.

It turned again, and they saw the unicorn's face had become thick, wide and reptilian. Two golden horns had grown out on either side of the spiky pink ones. It let out a deep, earthy roar that shook the streetlights. The unicorn had become a pink and gold dragon.

"Hurry!" Dred shouted to Mitch.

"I can't think of what to play!" Mitch said.

"Something about rain, maybe?" Erin suggested. She blew on her harmonica, and a breeze swept through the alley.

Mitch played the melody for the Eurythmics' "Here Comes the Rain Again." A huge, dense blue cloud filled the upper reaches of the alley, blocking their view of the dragon. A heavy downpour began immediately.

Jason knelt in the street, trying to pry open his guitar case. One of the latches was stuck. He must have closed it carelessly in the rush to pack up their things. He kept looking up at the sky through the rain, wondering where the dragon would reappear.

"Mitch, a storm!" Dred shouted. "Not just a little rain! Not even purple rain!"

Mitch switched over to a classical song. "Tchaikovsky," he said. "Number Five."

"Whatever!" Dred said.

The clouds filling the alley swelled and turned black. Balls of lightning bounced and crackled between the buildings, and the rain turned to hard, pelting hail.

The pink dragon came barreling down through the clouds, its jaws aimed right at Erin's head, as if it was following the sound of her harmonica.

Erin looked up and saw the pink reptilian face rushing down at her through the blinding rain and hail. She didn't see the big claw coming up behind her, the talon extended to hook through her as if the dragon planned to pick her up by her rib cage.

"Erin!" Jason yelled. He dove behind her, blocking the dragon's foot. One huge claw ripped diagonally across his back, slashing him open. He tumbled to the pavement with Erin in his arms. Her harmonica skittered away through the falling ice. Erin pulled free of him and crawled after it.

The dragon's claw turned Jason over on his back. Its maw breathed smoldering hot air in his face, and it glared at him with dark, angry eyes.

For some reason, all he could say was, "You're a unicorn."

The dragon's head curled back and its jaw widened, and it looked ready to bite his head off.

Erin blew a long, deep note on her harmonica, blowing a stiff wind up into one of the dragon's wings. The dragon tilted over to one side, and Erin threw herself across Jason so she could blow wind into both its wings at the same time.

The dragon's wings acted like sails, lifting the dragon high into the air. The tip of one claw cut Jason's ear and scratched along his head as the dragon soared out of reach.

The black clouds lashed the dragon with hail and lightning as it twisted and roared above them, jetting out a stream of fire. It started fighting its way down against the wind.

Jason crawled to his case and pulled at the jammed latch again. Then he turned the case on its side and bashed it against the street, breaking the latch altogether. The case fell open, and he caught his guitar by the neck as it tumbled toward the pavement.

Jason stood up, squinting against the rain as he found the bright shape of the dragon wriggling in and out of the swirling black clouds. He began to play. His guitar still felt hot, still charged up from the concert.

The rain turned to steam around him, and he played faster and harder as the dragon clawed its way down towards them.

He felt again the heat building all around him. He wanted to hit the dragon with all the power the guitar had. He kept playing, switching to the guitar riff from "Light My Fire" as if to really drive the point home. The guitar wasn't doing the work for him now. Jason had to make this happen himself.

He played until the air around him was scorching hot. The dragon managed to fold in its wings, and it dove straight for Erin.

Jason struck all six strings and released the heat bubble, with the face of his guitar pointed directly at the dragon. A giant fireball raced away from him, punching a wormhole of steam through the sheets of falling hail.

It struck the dragon and ignited, casting off blazing comets that sliced up the black clouds.

The dragon roared as the flames swept over it and engulfed its entire body. It plummeted towards them.

Jason dropped his guitar and grabbed Erin's hand, and they ran away together, toward the huge crowd of fans that had gathered behind the club and now gaped at the burning dragon falling towards the street.

The dragon's colossal body crashed to the ground, sending a wave of the shattered asphalt high into the air. Jason and Erin toppled over, and so did most of the gathered crowd.

The flames slowly twisted into dark smoke, as did the dragon body itself, leaving a dark heap of pink smoke behind. The stormclouds began to break up, and shafts of neon light from the Fleet Farm billboard above crept into the alley.

Jason helped Erin to her feet. Mitch and Dred sat up nearby—they'd run, too, abandoning their instruments. Everybody was covered in smoldering pink soot.

A tiny unicorn horn tumbled down through the smoke and clinked against the asphalt.

The audience burst into applause and whistles. Mitch waved, nodding, soaking it up.

Erin looked back at the drift of pink ash snowing down over their instruments. Then she looked at Jason.

"So...did we just kill a dragon?" she asked.

"I think so."

"That's more excitement than I expected in Minneapolis." She frowned and touched his cheek. "It got you pretty bad, didn't it?"

"Yeah, how's it look?" Jason turned around so she could where the dragon claw had raked his back. When he faced her again, she looked like she would burst into tears.

"Jason, I was talking about your *ear*," she said. "I didn't know about that."

"I got it when I saved your life from that dragon," he said. "Remember that?"

"I think I do." Erin stood on her tiptoes and gave him a long kiss.

"Buttercake!" the elf's voice wailed.

The rough-looking elf with the impossibly long name knelt in the pink ash, clutching the unicorn horn and weeping. "Poor, sweet Buttercake!" he cried.

Grizlemor strolled out from behind a dented trashcan, looking shocked.

"You beat the dragon?" the goblin asked Jason.

"Yeah," Jason said. "By the way, nice job mentioning that unicorns turn into dragons. Before you ran off."

"I thought everyone knew that," Grizlemor said.

"Now I'll have to take her back to the swamp and regrow her!" the elf cried, waving the horn at them. "I hope you're happy!" He turned and ran away into the dissolving pink smoke.

"Should we go catch that elf?" Jason asked.

"If you don't, he'll be able to tell the fairies about you," Grizlemor said.

Jason and Erin pursued the elf down to a sewer grate at the end of the alley. He slipped into the drain under the sidewalk, an opening much too narrow for either of them to follow him. They heard his footsteps splash away.

"I can't even think about chasing him," Erin said. "I'm about to collapse."

"Me, too."

They walked back up the alley together.

Mitch and Dred were busy with the crowd, who advanced further into the alley now, taking pictures and begging for autographs.

"I wonder if that dragon will be all over YouTube tomorrow," Erin said.

"It'd make a great video," Jason said. "Maybe you should write a song about it."

"Maybe you should," Erin replied. She squeezed his hand, then went to check on Mitch and Dred. The fans flooded around Jason, hugging him and taking pictures. He felt dazed, but he managed to smile.

Chapter Twenty-Seven

They dusted off their instruments and managed to drive away as the fire department arrived. Dred's van rode uneven and bumpy now, after being quaked hard by her drum, but it still drove.

They were quiet as they made their way out of Minneapolis. Mitch played the Rolling Stones on the stereo, and Dred didn't stop him.

"Dragonslayers," Grizlemor said, shaking his head. He sat on the heap of pink-dusted instrument cases behind them. "Queen Mab will have a new respect for you. Which isn't necessarily a good thing."

"I told you guys the fairies were nothing to worry about," Jason said.

"You call getting attacking by a giant candy dragon nothing to worry about?" Dred asked.

"Grizlemor," Mitch said. "I'd like to ask you a few things."

"Such as?"

"Things about being a goblin, basically."

"Ah. I happen to be a learned scholar on the subject." Grizlemor puffed his way from the back of the van to the front. He sat on the dashboard, dangling his feet while he answered Mitch and Dred's questions about goblins, fairies, elves and unicorn-dragons.

"How's your back?" Erin asked Jason. "Shouldn't we go to a hospital?"

"Nope, I'm fine. It's just a scratch." A diagonal streak of pain burned across his back where the dragon had clawed him. It did hurt, but he didn't want to complain. He wanted to get home.

Jason and Erin looked at each other, smiling. He took her hand, and she let him hold it for a minute. Then she slowly pulled away and gazed at the night outside her window. Her reflection showed a confused look. She would be thinking about her boyfriend, the one who was too busy shooting a German pizzeria commercial to see her first show.

But she had kissed him, and Jason knew she didn't hate him. Far from it.

Jason closed his eyes. Despite the aching wound in his back, he gradually dozed off as he rode home, and he dreamed of fairies, and of music, and of Erin.

THE END

ABOUT THE AUTHOR

J.L. Bryan studied English literature at the University of Georgia and at Oxford, with a focus on the English Renaissance and the Romantic period. He also studied screenwriting at UCLA. He enjoys remixing elements of paranormal, supernatural, fantasy, horror and science fiction into new kinds of stories. He is the author of The Paranormals trilogy (*Jenny Pox*, *Tommy Nightmare*, and *Alexander Death*), the biopunk sf novel *Helix*, and other works. *Fairy Metal Thunder* is the first book in his new Songs of Magic series. He lives in Atlanta with his wife Christina, one baby, two dogs, and two cats. His website is http://jlbryanbooks.com. You can also follow on him on Twitter (@jlbryanbooks) or Facebook.

Watch for:

FAIRY BLUES

SONGS OF MAGIC, BOOK 2

December 2011

9595617R0012

Made in the USA
Charleston, SC
25 September 2011